Resilience of the Heart

Elizabeth Ruthanne Martin

RESILIENCE OF THE HEART

Title Page

Resilience of the Heart:
Shadows of Betrayal

By: Elizabeth Ruthanne Martin

Book Summary

Newlyweds Isabella and Devin's honeymoon on a secluded Caribbean Island turns into a nightmare when Isabella receives a mysterious phone call revealing unsettling secrets about Trevor, a dark figure from her past. The caller hints at a powerful, unseen force pulling the strings behind Trevor's actions. Meanwhile, Trevor, seething with rage in prison, orchestrates a daring escape with the help of his ally, Jamie. Once free, Trevor plots a meticulous revenge against Isabella by targeting her charitable foundation, Bella's Haven.

Trevor's relentless attacks force Isabella out of hiding, leading to her capture and a chilling confrontation where Trevor vows to break her spirit. Devin, frantic over Isabella's disappearance, partners with Jamie to locate and rescue her. The ensuing battle in a dimly lit warehouse is intense and desperate, culminating in Isabella's escape and a dramatic intervention by the authorities. Despite the chaos and danger, Isabella and Devin's love and resilience shine through as they confront Trevor's malevolent schemes.

"Shadows of Deception" is a gripping tale of love, betrayal, and revenge, where enduring love faces off against a vengeful adversary, and resilience is the key to overcoming the darkest challenges.

1

A New Dawn

The first light of dawn began to pierce the horizon, casting a golden glow over the restful island. The peaceful atmosphere concealed the confusion within Isabella as she stood on the balcony of their honeymoon suite. The wedding had been a beautiful celebration of love and resilience, a testament to the strength of Isabella and Devin's bond. But now, in the soft morning light, she felt a profound sense of terror. Devin stood beside her, his arm wrapped around her waist, both of them basking in the moment's tranquility. "Can you believe we're finally here?" Isabella asked, her voice filled with wonder and a hint of lingering apprehension. Devin smiled, pressing a kiss to her temple. "It's been a long journey, Bella. But we've made it."

Their honeymoon destination was a secluded island in the Caribbean, chosen for its privacy and breathtaking beauty. It was a place where they could escape from the world and focus merely on each other, leaving behind the shadows of their past. The days passed in a blissful haze of sunshine, laughter, and love. They spent their mornings walking along the beach, their afternoons exploring the island, and their evenings enjoying intimate dinners under the stars. It was a time of healing and renewal, a chance to strengthen the unbreakable bond they shared. One afternoon, as they lounged on the beach, Devin turned to Isabella, his eyes filled with affection. "I have a surprise for you." She raised an eyebrow, curiosity piqued. "Oh? What is it?" Devin reached into his bag and pulled out a small, intricately carved box. "Open it." Isabella took the box, her heart racing with anticipation. She carefully lifted the lid, revealing a beautiful locket. Inside was a picture of their family—Isabella, Devin, Sophia, and their newborn son, Marco.

"It's beautiful, Devin," she said, tears filling her eyes. "Thank you." He smiled, taking the locket and fastening it around her neck. "I wanted you to have something to remind you of our family, no matter where we are." Isabella leaned into him, feeling a deep sense of love and gratitude. "I love you so much, Devin." "I love you too, Bella," he whispered, kissing her gently. Their honeymoon continued in a blissful routine, each day bringing new memories and deeper connections. One evening, as they enjoyed a quiet dinner on their private terrace, Isabella's phone buzzed with a notification. She glanced at the screen, her heart skipping a beat when she saw an unknown number. "I need to take this," she said, excusing herself from the table.

Devin nodded, watching her with a concerned expression as she walked to the edge of the terrace to take the call. "Hello?" she answered, her voice unsettled. "Isabella?" The voice on the other end was unfamiliar, yet there was a strange, unsettling familiarity to it. "Who is this?" she asked, her heart pounding with anxiety. There was a pause, and then the voice replied, "It's someone from your past. Someone who has information you need to know." Isabella's breath caught in her throat. "What kind of information?" "Something that could change everything," the voice said cryptically. "Meet me at the old lighthouse on the northern tip of the island tomorrow at noon. Come alone." Before Isabella could respond, the call disconnected, leaving her with a sense of uneasiness and confusion. She returned back to the table, her mind racing with questions. Devin looked up as she approached, concern etched on his face. "Is everything okay, Bella?" She forced a smile, trying to mask her unease. "Yeah, it was just... a wrong number." Devin reached for her hand, his eyes searching hers. "Are you sure? You seem shaken." Isabella nodded, squeezing his hand. "I'm fine, really. Let's just enjoy the rest of our evening."

But as they continued their dinner, the mysterious phone call lingered in Isabella's mind, casting a shadow over the evening. The next morning, Isabella woke early, her mind still preoccupied with the strange call. She decided to keep the meeting a secret from Devin, not wanting to worry him. As they enjoyed breakfast on the terrace, she made an excuse to explore the island on her own. "There's a lighthouse on the northern tip of the island," she said casually. "I'd love to go see it." Devin smiled, nodding. "Sounds like a great idea. Do you want me to come with you?" She shook her head, her heart heavy with the secret she was keeping. "No, I think I'd like to go alone. I need some time to reflect." Devin looked at her thoughtfully, then nodded. "Okay, Bella. Just be careful." Isabella kissed him, feeling a pang of guilt. "I will. I'll be back soon."

As she set off towards the lighthouse, her mind raced with anticipation and dread. What could this mysterious caller want? What information could they possibly have that would change everything? The journey to the lighthouse was long and difficult, the path winding through dense forests and rocky cliffs. Isabella's heart pounded with every step, her anxiety growing with each passing minute. When she finally reached the lighthouse, she found it deserted, its towering structure casting a long shadow over the rocky shore. She stood at the base, her eyes scanning the horizon for any sign of the mysterious caller. Suddenly, a figure emerged from the shadows, walking towards her with a purposeful stride. Isabella's breath caught in her throat as she recognized the face—a face she hadn't seen in years.

"Hello, Isabella," the figure said, their voice filled with a mix of familiarity and menace. Isabella took a step back, her heart racing. "What are you doing here? How did you find me?" The figure smiled, a cold, calculating smile. "I have my ways. And I have something you need to hear." Isabella's mind raced, her instincts screaming for her to run. But she stood her ground, determined to get answers. "What is it? What do you want?" The figure's expression darkened; their eyes gleaming with a sinister light. "I want to tell you the truth about Trevor. And about your family." A chill ran down Isabella's spine as the figure's words sunk in. "What do you mean?" The figure stepped closer, their voice dropping to a whisper. "Trevor wasn't working alone. There's someone else—someone powerful—who has been pulling the strings all along."

Isabella's heart pounded in her chest as the figure continued. "And that someone is still out there, watching your every move." Before Isabella could respond, the figure turned and disappeared into the shadows, leaving her with more questions than answers. She stood there, her mind reeling, as the weight of the revelation settled over her. As she made her way back to the villa, her thoughts were a whirlwind of confusion and fear. Who was this mysterious figure? And what did they mean by someone else was pulling the strings? When she finally reached the villa, she found Devin waiting for her, his expression filled with concern. "Bella, are you okay? You were gone for a long time." Isabella forced a smile, her mind racing with the secrets she now carried. "I'm fine, Devin. Just needed some time to think."

But as they embraced, Isabella couldn't shake the feeling that their lives were about to change once again. The mysterious phone call had opened a door to a new, unsettling reality, and she knew that the answers she needed would come at a price. As the sun set over the horizon, casting a golden glow over the island, Isabella and Devin sat together on the balcony, holding each other close. The future was uncertain, but their love remained a constant, unbreakable bond. Isabella looked out at the ocean, her mind filled with questions and fears. The mysterious caller's words echoed in her mind, a haunting reminder that their journey was far from over. Devin sensed her unease, his grip tightening around her. "Whatever it is, Bella, we'll face it together. You and me, against the world." She nodded, finding strength in his words. "Together."

As the stars began to twinkle in the night sky, Isabella knew that their story was far from finished. The shadows of their past still lingered, and new challenges awaited them. But with Devin by her side, she was ready to face whatever lay ahead. And as the waves crashed against the shore, a sense of resolve settled over her. They had overcome so much already, and she knew they would find the strength to face whatever darkness still lay in their path. For now, they would hold onto their love, their hope, and the promise of a brighter future. And as they watched the stars together, Isabella felt a glimmer of hope, knowing that they would face the shadows together, no matter what. As they stood on the balcony, holding each other close, the phone buzzed once again. Isabella's heart skipped a beat as she glanced at the screen. It was another unknown number. With a sense of uneasiness, she answered the call. "Hello?"

The voice on the other end was different this time, more urgent. "Isabella, this is important. You need to know the truth." Isabella's breath caught in her throat as the voice continued, "There's more at stake than you realize. Meet me at the old pier tomorrow at noon. And come alone." The call disconnected, leaving Isabella with a sense of dread and anticipation. She looked at Devin, her mind racing with the implications of the call. "Who was it?" Devin asked, his eyes filled with concern. Isabella hesitated, knowing that the next steps they took could change everything. "It was... someone with more information about Trevor. They want to meet tomorrow."

Devin's expression hardened with determination. "Then we'll go together." Isabella shook her head, her voice firm. "No, Devin. This is something I need to do on my own." He looked at her, worry etched on his face. "Bella, I don't like the idea of you going alone. What if it's a trap?" She placed a reassuring hand on his cheek. "I'll be careful. I promise. But I need to know what's going on. I need to face this." Devin sighed, his protective instincts warring with his understanding of her need for independence. "Alright, Bella. But I'll be nearby. If anything goes wrong, call me immediately." Isabella nodded, feeling a mix of gratitude and guilt. "Thank you, Devin. I love you." "I love you too, Bella," he said, pulling her into a tight embrace. "Be careful."

The next day, Isabella set off for the old pier, her heart heavy with anticipation. The journey was long, her mind racing with thoughts of the mysterious caller and the secrets they held. As she walked along the path, she couldn't shake the feeling that she was being watched. When she reached the pier, she found it deserted, the wooden planks creaking under her feet. She looked around, her senses heightened by the tension. A figure emerged from the shadows, walking towards her with a purposeful stride. Isabella's breath caught in her throat as she recognized the face—a face she hadn't seen in years. "Hello, Isabella," the figure said, their voice filled with a mix of familiarity and menace. Isabella took a step back, her heart racing. "What are you doing here? How did you find me?" The figure smiled, a cold, calculating smile. "I have my ways. And I have something you need to hear."

Isabella's mind raced, her instincts screaming for her to run. But she stood her ground, determined to get answers. "What is it? What do you want?" The figure's expression darkened; their eyes gleaming with a sinister light. "I want to tell you the truth about Trevor. And about your family." A chill ran down Isabella's spine as the figure's words sunk in. "What do you mean?" The figure stepped closer, their voice dropping to a whisper. "Trevor wasn't working alone. There's someone else—someone powerful—who has been pulling the strings all along." Isabella's heart pounded in her chest as the figure continued. "And that someone is still out there, watching your every move."

Before Isabella could respond, the figure turned and disappeared into the shadows, leaving her with more questions than answers. She stood there, her mind reeling, as the weight of the revelation settled over her. As she made her way back to the villa, her thoughts were a whirlwind of confusion and fear. Who was this mysterious figure? And what did they mean by someone else was pulling the strings? When she finally reached the villa, she found Devin waiting for her, his expression filled with concern. "Bella, are you okay? You were gone for a long time." Isabella forced a smile, her mind racing with the secrets she now carried. "I'm fine, Devin. Just needed some time to think."

But as they embraced, Isabella couldn't shake the feeling that their lives were about to change once again. The mysterious phone call had opened a door to a new, unsettling reality, and she knew that the answers she needed would come at a price. As the sun set over the horizon, casting a golden glow over the island, Isabella and Devin sat together on the balcony, holding each other close. The future was uncertain, but their love remained a constant, unbreakable bond. Isabella looked out at the ocean, her mind filled with questions and fears. The mysterious caller's words echoed in her mind, a haunting reminder that their journey was far from over. Devin sensed her unease, his grip tightening around her. "Whatever it is, Bella, we'll face it together. You and me, against the world." She nodded, finding strength in his words. "Together."

As the stars began to twinkle in the night sky, Isabella knew that their story was far from finished. The shadows of their past still lingered, and new challenges awaited them. But with Devin by her side, she was ready to face whatever lay ahead. And as the waves crashed against the shore, a sense of resolve settled over her. They had overcome so much already, and she knew they would find the strength to face whatever darkness still lay in their path. For now, they would hold onto their love, their hope, and the promise of a brighter future. And as they watched the stars together, Isabella felt a glimmer of hope, knowing that they would face the shadows together, no matter what. As they stood on the balcony, holding each other close, the phone buzzed once again. Isabella's heart skipped a beat as she glanced at the screen. It was another unknown number. With a sense of uneasiness, she answered the call. "Hello?"

The voice on the other end was different this time, more urgent. "Isabella, this is important. You need to know the truth." Isabella's breath caught in her throat as the voice continued, "There's more at stake than you realize. Meet me at the old pier tomorrow at noon.

And come alone." The call disconnected, leaving Isabella with a sense of dread and anticipation. She looked at Devin, her mind racing with the implications of the call. "Who was it?" Devin asked, his eyes filled with concern. Isabella hesitated, knowing that the next steps they took could change everything. "It was... someone with more information about Trevor. They want to meet tomorrow." Devin's expression hardened with determination. "Then we'll go together." Isabella shook her head, her voice firm. "No, Devin. This is something I need to do on my own."

He looked at her, worry etched on his face. "Bella, I don't like the idea of you going alone. What if it's a trap?" She placed a reassuring hand on his cheek. "I'll be careful. I promise. But I need to know what's going on. I need to face this." Devin sighed, his protective instincts warring with his understanding of her need for independence. "Alright, Bella. But I'll be nearby. If anything goes wrong, call me immediately." Isabella nodded, feeling a mix of gratitude and guilt. "Thank you, Devin. I love you." "I love you too, Bella," he said, pulling her into a tight embrace. "Be careful." The next day, Isabella set off for the old pier, her heart heavy with anticipation. The journey was long, her mind racing with thoughts of the mysterious caller and the secrets they held. As she walked along the path, she couldn't shake the feeling that she was being watched.

When she reached the pier, she found it deserted, the wooden planks creaking under her feet. She looked around, her senses heightened by the tension. A figure emerged from the shadows, walking towards her with a purposeful stride. Isabella's breath caught in her throat as she recognized the face—a face she hadn't seen in years. "Hello, Isabella," the figure said, their voice filled with a mix of familiarity and menace. Isabella took a step back, her heart racing. "What are you doing here? How did you find me?" The figure smiled, a cold, calculating smile. "I have my ways. And I have something you need to hear." Isabella's mind raced, her instincts screaming for her to run. But she stood her ground, determined to get answers. "What is it? What do you want?" The figure's expression darkened; their eyes gleaming with a sinister light. "I want to tell you the truth about Trevor. And about your family."

A chill ran down Isabella's spine as the figure's words sunk in. "What do you mean?" The figure stepped closer, their voice dropping to a whisper. "Trevor wasn't working alone. There's someone else—someone powerful—who has been pulling the strings all along." Isabella's heart pounded in her chest as the figure continued. "And that someone is still out there, watching your every move." Before Isabella could respond, the figure turned and disappeared into the shadows, leaving her with more questions than answers. She stood there, her mind reeling, as the weight of the revelation settled over her. As she made her way back to the villa, her thoughts were a whirlwind of confusion and fear. Who was this mysterious figure? And what did they mean by someone else was pulling the strings?

When she finally reached the villa, she found Devin waiting for her, his expression filled with concern. "Bella, are you okay? You were gone for a long time." Isabella forced a smile, her mind racing with the secrets she now carried. "I'm fine, Devin. Just needed some time to think." But as they embraced, Isabella couldn't shake the feeling that their lives were about to change once again. The mysterious phone call had opened a door to a new, unsettling reality, and she knew that the answers she needed would come at a price. As the sun set over the horizon, casting a golden glow over the island, Isabella and Devin sat together on the balcony, holding each other close. The future was uncertain, but their love remained a constant, unbreakable bond.

Isabella looked out at the ocean, her mind filled with questions and fears. The mysterious caller's words echoed in her mind, a haunting reminder that their journey was far from over. Devin sensed her unease, his grip tightening around her. "Whatever it is, Bella, we'll face it together. You and me, against the world." She nodded, finding strength in his words. "Together." As the stars began to twinkle in the night sky, Isabella knew that their story was far from finished.

The shadows of their past still lingered, and new challenges awaited them. But with Devin by her side, she was ready to face whatever lay ahead. And as the waves crashed against the shore, a sense of resolve settled over her. They had overcome so much already, and she knew they would find the strength to face whatever darkness still lay in their path. For now, they would hold onto their love, their hope, and the promise of a brighter future. And as they watched the stars together, Isabella felt a glimmer of hope, knowing that they would face the shadows together, no matter what.

2

Trevor's Rage

Trevor sat on the edge of his narrow bed, the cold steel frame digging into his back as he stared at the concrete wall of his cell. The dim light from the small window cast long shadows, highlighting the harshness of his surroundings. The pulsing chime of the prison bars echoed through the corridors, a constant reminder of his confinement. But it wasn't the cold or the confinement that gnawed at him; it was the burning rage that simmered just beneath the surface.

Isabella. The name alone sent a wave of fury coursing through him. She had outsmarted him again, slipped through his fingers like a wisp of smoke. He clenched his fists, his knuckles turning white. How had she managed to do it? How had she turned the tables on him so completely? He had been so close. His plan had been precise, every detail accounted for. Yet, she had found a way to escape, to expose him, and now he was here, rotting in this godforsaken place. The thought of her living her life, free and happy, while he was trapped in this cage was unbearable. The guards patrolled the corridors, their heavy footsteps a constant reminder of his captivity. Trevor's mind raced, replaying the events that had led him here. He had underestimated her, underestimated her resilience and strength. But he wouldn't make that mistake again. No, next time he would be ready.

He had spent countless hours analyzing every move, every decision that had brought him to this point. The betrayal, the deception, it all fueled his determination. He had allies, powerful ones, who had promised to help him. But even they couldn't protect him from his own failures. "Hey, Trevor," a voice called from the adjacent cell, breaking the silence. "What's got you so worked up?" Trevor didn't bother to look. He knew the voice belonged to Joe; a fellow inmate who had been locked up for armed robbery. Joe was always looking for gossip, a way to pass the time. Trevor had no intention of indulging him. "None of your business," Trevor replied, his voice cold and dismissive. Joe chuckled. "Come on, man. We're all in the same boat here. What's eating at you?" Trevor sighed, running a hand through his hair. "Just thinking about how I ended up in this shithole." Joe leaned closer to the bars that separated their cells. "Let me guess, a woman?" Trevor's eyes narrowed. "How did you know?" Joe laughed, a hollow, bitter sound. "It's always a woman, isn't it? They get under your skin, mess with your head. So, what's her story?"

Trevor hesitated, but then the words spilled out, fueled by his anger. "Her name's Isabella. She ruined everything. I had it all planned out, and she destroyed it." Joe nodded sympathetically. "Women have a way of doing that. What did she do?" Trevor's jaw tightened. "She exposed me, got me locked up in here. But she's not going to get away with it. I'll make sure of that." Joe's eyes gleamed with interest. "Got a plan?" Trevor's lips curled into a sinister smile. "Oh, I've got a plan. And when I get out of here, she'll regret the day she ever crossed me." The days turned into weeks, and Trevor's rage only grew stronger. He spent his time plotting, coming up with a way to turn the tables once more. He knew he had to bide his time, wait for the right moment. But he would get his revenge, and when he did, Isabella would pay.

One afternoon, as he was being escorted back to his cell from the yard, Trevor overheard a conversation between two guards. They were talking about an upcoming transfer, a move that would place him in a higher security facility. Trevor's heart sank. If he was moved, it would make his escape nearly impossible. He needed to act fast. That night, as the prison lights dimmed for lights-out, Trevor lay on his bed, staring at the ceiling. He couldn't afford to wait any longer.

He needed to contact his allies, set his plan into motion. But first, he had to find a way to get a message out. The next morning, during breakfast, Trevor spotted a familiar face in the cafeteria. It was Mike, a low-level enforcer who owed him a favor. Trevor made his way over to Mike's table, sitting down without invitation. "Mike," he said, keeping his voice low. "I need your help." Mike looked up; his eyes wary. "What do you want, Trevor?" "I need you to get a message to someone on the outside. It's urgent."

Mike hesitated, glancing around the room. "You know that's risky. If we get caught..." Trevor leaned in closer, his eyes burning with intensity. "I don't care about the risks. This is important. Do it, and I'll make sure you're taken care of when I get out." Mike considered for a moment, then nodded reluctantly. "Alright, what's the message?" Trevor quickly scribbled a note on a piece of paper, folding it tightly. "Get this to Jamie. He'll know what to do." Mike took the note, slipping it into his pocket. "I'll do my best." As the days passed, Trevor's anxiety grew. He watched and waited, hoping that his message had made it to Jamie. He knew that Jamie had the resources and connections to help him, but time was running out. One evening, as Trevor was lying in his cell, the guard approached with a note. "You got a message, Trevor." Trevor's heart raced as he took the note, unfolding it quickly. The message was brief but promising: "Plans in motion. Stay strong."

Relief washed over him. Jamie had received his message and was working on a plan. Now, all Trevor had to do was wait for the right moment to make his move. Days turned into weeks, and the tension in the prison grew visible. Trevor could sense that something was about to happen. He kept a low profile, avoiding trouble, knowing that any misstep could jeopardize his plan. Then, one night, the sound of alarms shattered the stillness. Trevor's heart pounded as he realized that this was it—the moment he had been waiting for. He sprang into action, following the plan that had been carefully laid out. As chaos erupted around him, Trevor made his way through the prison, avoiding guards and navigating the labyrinthine corridors.

He reached the rendezvous point, where Jamie's men were waiting. "Let's go," one of them said, handing Trevor a set of keys. Trevor didn't hesitate. He followed them through a series of tunnels, emerging outside the prison walls. The cool night air was a stark contrast to the stifling confinement he had endured. "Get in," Jamie's man said, opening the door to a waiting vehicle. Trevor climbed in, his mind racing with thoughts of revenge. As the car sped away from the prison, he knew that his freedom was just the beginning. He had a score to settle, and nothing would stand in his way. The drive was long, but Trevor's mind was focused. He knew exactly what he needed to do. Isabella had ruined his plans, but he would make sure she paid dearly for it.

When they finally arrived at a safe house, Trevor stepped out of the car, taking a deep breath. He turned to Jamie, who was waiting for him. "Welcome back," Jamie said, a knowing smile on his face. "Thanks," Trevor replied, his voice cold and determined. "Now, let's get to work." As they entered the safe house, Trevor felt a renewed sense of purpose. He was free, and he had a plan. Isabella had outsmarted him once, but she wouldn't do it again. He would find her, and he would make her suffer for every moment of his captivity. In the dim light of the safe house, Trevor began to outline his strategy, his mind sharp and focused. He knew that this time, he had to be smarter, more ruthless. There was no room for error.

And so, with Jamie's help, Trevor began to rebuild his network, gathering allies and resources. He knew that the road ahead would be difficult, but he was determined. Isabella had escaped his grasp once, but he would make sure it never happened again. As the days turned into weeks, Trevor's plan took shape. He was patient, biding his time, waiting for the perfect moment to strike. And when that moment came, he would be ready. Isabella had no idea what was coming. Trevor's rage had transformed into a cold, calculated resolve. He would stop at nothing to see his plans through, and nothing would stand in his way. As the first light of dawn began to pierce the horizon, Trevor stood at the window of the safe house, his mind filled with thoughts of revenge. The peaceful atmosphere concealed the storm that was brewing within him. He had been beaten, but he was far from broken. And he would make sure that Isabella knew the full extent of his wrath.

3

The Plan

The safe house was quiet, the air thick with anticipation. Trevor paced back and forth, his mind racing with thoughts of revenge and retribution. The dim light from the single bulb hanging from the ceiling cast eerie shadows on the walls, amplifying the ominous atmosphere. Jamie sat at the makeshift table in the center of the room, watching Trevor with a mixture of curiosity and concern. "So, what's the plan, Trevor? How are we going to get Isabella back?" Trevor paused, his eyes narrowing as he considered his next move. He had been carefully planning his revenge, every detail accounted for. Isabella had outsmarted him once, but she wouldn't do it again. He would make sure of that. "We start by gathering intel," Trevor said, his voice cold and determined. "I need to know everything about her—where she is, what she's doing, who she's with. We need to find her weaknesses and exploit them." Jamie nodded, pulling out a laptop and powering it up. "I've already started digging into her recent activities. She's been busy with Bella's Haven, expanding to new locations. It seems like she's focused on helping others, but that makes her vulnerable. She can't protect everyone."

Trevor's lips curled into a sinister smile. "Good. We'll use that to our advantage. We'll hit her where it hurts the most—her precious foundation. If we can damage Bella's Haven, she'll come running to protect it." Jamie continued typing, pulling up a map of Bella's Haven locations. "There are several new centers in neighboring cities. We could target one of those." Trevor nodded, his mind racing with possibilities. "Yes. We'll start with the newest center. It will be the least protected and the easiest to disrupt. Once we have her attention, we can lure her into a trap." As Jamie worked on gathering more information, Trevor began outlining the details of their plan. They would need a team, people they could trust to carry out the operation without hesitation. Trevor made a list of names, individuals with the skills and loyalty he needed. "We'll need muscle, tech experts, and a few insiders who can get us information from the inside," Trevor said, handing the list to Jamie. "Start reaching out to these people. Make sure they understand the stakes."

Jamie nodded, taking the list and getting to work. Trevor's mind was a whirlwind of thoughts and strategies. He couldn't afford any mistakes. Isabella had to pay for what she had done, and he would stop at nothing to see it through. Over the next few days, Jamie and Trevor worked tirelessly to put their plan into motion. They contacted the individuals on Trevor's list, arranging secret meetings and securing their loyalty. Each person brought a unique skill set to the table, and Trevor was confident that they had the right team for the job. One evening, as the team gathered in the safe house, Trevor stood before them, his eyes gleaming with determination. "Listen up," he said, his voice commanding attention. "We have a mission—to bring Isabella to her knees. This isn't just about revenge. It's about taking back control and making sure she understands the consequences of crossing me."

The team nodded, their expressions a mix of seriousness and anticipation. They knew the risks, but they were ready to follow Trevor's lead. "Our first target is the new Bella's Haven center," Trevor continued. "We'll hit it hard and fast, create chaos and make sure Isabella knows who's behind it. Once we have her attention, we'll set the trap." The team spent hours going over the details of the plan, ensuring that every aspect was covered. They would strike at night, using the cover of darkness to their advantage. The tech experts would disable the security systems, while the muscle would handle any resistance. As the night of the operation approached, Trevor felt a sense of excitement building within him. This was it—the moment he had been waiting for. He could almost taste the satisfaction of seeing Isabella brought to her knees.

On the night of the operation, the team assembled at a prearranged location near the Bella's Haven center. The air was thick with tension, each member of the team focused and ready for action. "Remember, stick to the plan," Trevor said, his voice low and intense. "We go in, create chaos, and get out. No mistakes." The team nodded, and they moved into position. The tech experts worked quickly to disable the security systems, and within minutes, the center was plunged into darkness. Trevor and the muscle moved in, their footsteps silent and purposeful. They entered the building, their flashlights cutting through the darkness. The sound of breaking glass and overturned furniture filled the air as they created the chaos they needed. Trevor felt a rush of adrenaline as he watched the destruction unfold. "Move fast," he ordered, his voice barely above a whisper. "We don't have much time."

As they continued their rampage, Trevor's mind was already racing ahead to the next step. This was just the beginning. Once Isabella realized what was happening, she would have no choice but to come out of hiding. Suddenly, the sound of sirens filled the air. Trevor's heart raced as he realized their time was running out. "Let's go!" he shouted, leading the team back to their exit. They moved quickly, slipping out of the building and disappearing into the night. As they regrouped at the safe house, Trevor couldn't help but feel a sense of satisfaction. The operation had been a success, and now the real game could begin. The next morning, news of the attack on the Bella's Haven center spread like wildfire. Isabella's face was plastered across every news channel, her expression one of shock and determination. Trevor watched the reports with a cold smile, knowing that his plan was working.

"She's going to come after us," Jamie said, watching the news with a frown. "We need to be ready." Trevor nodded, his mind already working on the next phase of the plan. "We'll be ready. She won't see us coming." Over the next few days, Trevor and his team continued to disrupt Isabella's operations. They targeted other Bella's Haven centers, creating chaos and sending a clear message. Each attack brought them closer to their goal, and Trevor enjoyed the thought of Isabella's growing desperation. One evening, as they were planning their next move, Jamie received a call. He listened for a moment, then turned to Trevor with a serious expression. "We've got a lead on Isabella's location. She's staying at a safe house in the city."

Trevor's eyes gleamed with excitement. "Perfect. This is our chance." The team quickly mobilized, preparing for the final phase of their plan. They would capture Isabella and bring her to a location of their choosing, where Trevor would finally confront her. As they moved into position near the safe house, Trevor felt a mix of anticipation and satisfaction. This was it—the moment he had been waiting for. He would make Isabella pay for everything she had done. The team moved silently, surrounding the safe house and cutting off any escape routes. Trevor led the way, his heart pounding with excitement. As they approached the building, he motioned for the team to move in. They entered the safe house, their weapons at the ready. The sound of footsteps echoed through the corridors as they searched for Isabella. Trevor's mind raced with thoughts of revenge, his anger fueling his determination.

Finally, they found her. Isabella stood in the center of a dimly lit room, her eyes wide with fear and defiance. Trevor's heart raced as he stepped forward, his eyes locked on hers. "Hello, Isabella," he said, his voice cold and menacing. "It's been a long time." Isabella's eyes narrowed; her expression defiant. "Trevor. What do you want?" Trevor smiled, a cruel glint in his eyes. "I want you to understand the consequences of crossing me. I want you to feel the same pain and desperation you put me through." Isabella took a step back, her eyes filled with a mixture of fear and determination. "You won't get away with this, Trevor. People will come looking for me." Trevor's smile widened. "Let them come. It won't change a thing. You're mine now, Isabella." As he spoke, the team moved in, securing Isabella and preparing to transport her to their chosen location. Trevor watched with satisfaction, knowing that his plan was finally coming to fulfillment.

As they left the safe house, Trevor felt a sense of triumph. He had done it. He had captured Isabella, and now he would make her pay for everything she had done. The drive to their location was tense, the air thick with anticipation. Isabella sat silently; her eyes locked on Trevor. He could see the fear and determination in her eyes, and it only fueled his resolve. When they arrived at the location, a remote warehouse on the outskirts of the city, Trevor led Isabella inside. The team followed, securing the area and ensuring that they wouldn't be interrupted. Trevor turned to Isabella, his eyes cold and calculating. "This is where it ends, Isabella. This is where you learn the true meaning of consequences." Isabella met his gaze, her voice steady despite the fear in her eyes. "You're a monster, Trevor. You'll never break me." Trevor's smile widened, a cruel glint in his eyes. "We'll see about that." As he began to outline his plans for Isabella, the air grew thick with tension. The warehouse was silent, the only sound the faint hum of the lights overhead. Trevor's mind raced with thoughts of revenge, his anger and determination driving him forward.

He would make Isabella pay for everything she had done. He would break her spirit and ensure that she never crossed him again. And as he watched her, he knew that this was just the beginning. The game was far from over, and Trevor was ready to play it to the bitter end. As the night wore on, Trevor continued to lay out his plans, his voice cold and relentless. Isabella listened; her expression defiant but fearful. Trevor knew that he had the upper hand, and he was determined to see his plan through to the end. This was his moment of triumph, and he would savor every second of it. The dark and ominous atmosphere of the warehouse mirrored the darkness within him, a testament to the lengths he would go to for revenge. Trevor had waited a long time for this moment, and he was ready to take his revenge. Isabella had crossed him for the last time, and now she would pay the price. The night was far from over, and the game had only just begun.

4

Shadows of Desperation

Devin sat in the dimly lit living room; his hands clenched into fists. The room was silent except for the occasional creak of the old wooden floorboards. He couldn't shake the gnawing feeling of dread that had settled in his stomach ever since Isabella had gone missing. The authorities had been notified, but they had no leads. He had contacted everyone he could think of—friends, colleagues, and even Jamie, their trusted ally in the fight against Trevor. The image of Isabella's empty side of the bed haunted him. She had been there only hours ago, safe and sound, or so he had thought. Now, she was out there somewhere, taken by the man who had tormented them for so long. Devin's mind raced with thoughts of what Trevor could be doing to her, the unimaginable horrors that might be unfolding. He had to find her. He couldn't lose her, not after everything they had been through. Isabella's heart pounded in her chest as she sat in the dimly lit warehouse, her wrists bound to the chair she was seated in. Trevor's cold eyes drill into her, his lips curling into a sinister smile. She refused to let him see her fear, even though it threatened to consume her. She had to stay strong, for herself and for Devin. "You think you can break me, Trevor?" she spat, her voice steady despite the terror coursing through her veins. "You won't win." Trevor chuckled, a sound that sent chills down her spine. "We'll see about that, Isabella. You have no idea what I'm capable of."

The air was thick with tension, the darkness of the warehouse amplifying the sense of dread that hung over them. Isabella's mind raced with thoughts of escape, of finding a way to outsmart Trevor and get back to Devin. She knew he was looking for her, that he wouldn't rest until he found her. But time was running out, and she needed to act quickly. Devin paced the room, his mind racing with possibilities. He couldn't sit still, couldn't bear the thought of Isabella in danger. He picked up his phone and dialed Jamie's number once again, praying for an update. "Devin," Jamie's voice crackled through the line. "I've been tracking some leads. There's a warehouse on the outskirts of the city that matches the description of the place where Isabella might be held. I'm heading there now." Devin's heart leapt. "I'm coming with you." "Meet me there," Jamie instructed. "And be careful. We don't know what we're walking into." Devin hung up and grabbed his jacket, his resolve hardening. He would find Isabella and bring her home, no matter the cost.

Isabella's mind raced as she watched Trevor pace back and forth, his eyes gleaming with hatred. She had to find a way out, had to stay one step ahead of him. Her wrists ached from the tight bindings, but she ignored the pain, focusing on the task at hand. "You know, Trevor," she said, her voice calm and measured, "this isn't going to end well for you. Devin will find me. And when he does, you'll pay for everything you've done." Trevor's smile faltered for a moment, a flicker of uncertainty crossing his face. But he quickly regained his composure, his eyes narrowing. "You're delusional, Isabella. Devin can't save you this time." Isabella met his gaze, her eyes filled with determination. "We'll see about that." As Trevor turned his back to her, she began to work on the bindings, trying to loosen them enough to slip her hands free. Every second counted, and she couldn't afford to waste any of them.

Devin drove through the deserted streets, his heart pounding with a mix of fear and determination. The warehouse loomed ahead, its dark silhouette a beacon of hope and dread. He parked the car a short distance away and approached the building on foot, his senses heightened by the adrenaline coursing through his veins. He spotted Jamie waiting near the entrance, his expression grim. "Any sign of her?" Devin asked, his voice barely above a whisper. Jamie shook his head. "Not yet. But I have a feeling she's in there. We need to move quickly and quietly." Devin nodded; his mind focused on one thing: getting Isabella out of there safely. They crept towards the entrance, their movements silent and deliberate. The darkness of the warehouse blanketed them as they slipped inside, their flashlights casting eerie shadows on the walls.

Isabella's heart raced as she finally managed to loosen the bindings enough to free one of her hands. She worked quickly, untying the other hand and rising from the chair as silently as she could. She knew she had to be careful, that any noise could alert Trevor to her escape. She glanced around the dimly lit room, her eyes searching for anything she could use as a weapon. Her gaze settled on a metal pipe lying on the ground, and she quickly picked it up, gripping it tightly in her hands. She moved towards the door, her footsteps light and silent. Just as she reached the door, it swung open, revealing Trevor standing on the other side. His eyes widened in surprise, and Isabella didn't hesitate. She swung the pipe with all her strength, aiming for his head.

Trevor ducked just in time, the pipe missing him by inches. He lunged at her, his hands reaching for the pipe. Isabella struggled against him, her determination giving her strength. She couldn't let him win, couldn't let him take her again. Devin and Jamie moved through the warehouse, their flashlights cutting through the darkness. Devin's heart pounded in his chest; his mind filled with thoughts of Isabella. He had to find her, had to save her. Suddenly, they heard the sound of a struggle coming from a nearby room. Devin's heart leapt into his throat as he recognized Isabella's voice. He sprinted towards the sound; Jamie close behind him. They burst into the room to find Isabella and Trevor locked in a fierce struggle. Devin's eyes locked onto Isabella, her face pale but determined. He didn't hesitate, lunging at Trevor and tackling him to the ground.

"Isabella, run!" Devin shouted; his voice filled with urgency. Isabella hesitated for a moment, her eyes wide with fear and determination. She glanced at Devin, then turned and ran towards the exit, her heart pounding in her chest. Trevor struggled against Devin; his eyes filled with rage. "You think you can stop me?" he snarled; his voice filled with venom. Devin's grip tightened on Trevor; his determination unwavering. "I will stop you. You'll never hurt her again." Isabella's mind raced as she ran through the darkened corridors of the warehouse. She had to find a way out, had to escape before Trevor could catch up to her. Her breath came in ragged gasps, her heart pounding in her chest.

She stumbled through a doorway and found herself in a large, empty room. She looked around frantically, searching for an exit. Her eyes settled on a window high up on the wall, and she knew it was her only chance. She climbed onto a stack of crates, her hands shaking as she struggled to reach the window. She managed to pry it open and climbed through, dropping to the ground outside. The cool night air hit her like a wave, and she took a moment to catch her breath. She glanced back at the warehouse, her heart aching for Devin. She couldn't leave him behind, not after everything they had been through. She had to find help, had to get him out of there. Devin and Trevor continued to struggle, their movements a blur of violence and determination. Devin's mind was focused on one thing: keeping Trevor away from Isabella. He couldn't let him win, couldn't let him take her again.

Suddenly, Trevor managed to break free, his eyes filled with a wild, desperate rage. He lunged at Devin, his hands reaching for his throat. Devin fought back with all his strength, his determination giving him the upper hand. He managed to push Trevor away, his eyes locking onto his enemy's. "It's over, Trevor. You'll never hurt her again." Trevor's eyes narrowed; his voice filled with venom. "This isn't over,

Devin. I'll find her. I'll make you both pay." Devin's resolve hardened; his determination unwavering. "No, you won't. You'll never get near her again." As the struggle continued, Devin knew that he had to end this, had to stop Trevor once and for all. He couldn't let him win, couldn't let him take Isabella. He would fight with everything he had, and he would not stop until Trevor was defeated.

Isabella stumbled through the darkened streets, her mind racing with thoughts of Devin. She had to find help, had to get back to him. She couldn't leave him behind, not after everything they had been through. She spotted a police car parked on the corner and ran towards it, her breath coming in ragged gasps. She pounded on the window, her voice filled with desperation. "Please, you have to help me. My husband is in danger." The officer inside the car looked up, his eyes widening in surprise. He quickly stepped out of the car; his expression serious. "What's going on? Where is he?" Isabella pointed towards the warehouse, her hands shaking. "He's inside. He's fighting with the man who took me. You have to help him." The officer nodded, quickly radioing for backup. "Stay here. We'll get him out." Isabella watched as the officer ran towards the warehouse, her heart pounding in her chest. She prayed that Devin would be safe, that they would both make it out of this nightmare.

5

The Confrontation

Devin's heart pounded in his chest as he continued to struggle with Trevor. The dim light of the warehouse cast long, eerie shadows that seemed to move with a life of their own. Devin's mind raced with thoughts of Isabella, praying that she had found safety and that help was on its way. Trevor's eyes gleamed with a deranged intensity; his movements fueled by a twisted determination. Devin could see the hatred in his eyes, the cold calculation that had driven Trevor to torment their lives. This was a man who would stop at nothing to get what he wanted.

"You think you can stop me?" Trevor snarled, his voice dripping with venom. "Isabella will never be safe as long as I'm alive. I'll get to her, one way or another." Devin's grip tightened, his resolve hardening. "Over my dead body," he spat back, his voice filled with defiance. Trevor's lips curled into a sinister smile. "That can be arranged." With a surge of strength, Trevor broke free from Devin's grasp and lunged at him with renewed fury. The two men clashed in a violent struggle, their movements a blur of fists and rage. Devin fought with everything he had, but Trevor's relentless assault began to take its toll. Trevor managed to land a vicious punch to Devin's jaw, sending him staggering backwards. Devin tried to regain his footing, but Trevor was on him in an instant, his hands wrapped around Devin's throat. The pressure was suffocating, and Devin's vision began to blur. "You're weak," Trevor hissed, his grip tightening. "You can't protect her. You never could."

Devin's mind flashed with images of Isabella, her face filled with fear and determination. He couldn't let Trevor win. He had to fight for her, for their future. Summoning every ounce of strength he had left; Devin managed to twist his body and break free from Trevor's hold. Gasping for breath, Devin scrambled to his feet, his eyes locked on Trevor. "I'll never let you take her," he said, his voice hoarse but unwavering. Trevor's smile faded, replaced by a look of cold determination. "We'll see about that." The two men circled each other, the tension in the air noticeable. Devin could feel the weight of the confrontation bearing down on him, the sense of impending dread that hung over them like a dark cloud.

He knew that this battle was about more than just physical strength—it was a test of wills, a fight for the very soul of their lives. Trevor feinted to the left, then lunged to the right, his movements quick and calculated. Devin barely managed to block the attack, but Trevor's next strike caught him off guard, sending him crashing to the ground. Pain shot through Devin's body, but he refused to give up. As Devin struggled to get back on his feet, Trevor loomed over him, his eyes filled with a twisted satisfaction. "You're finished, Devin. And when I'm done with you, I'll find Isabella. She'll never be free of me." Devin's heart ached with a mixture of fear and fury. He couldn't let Trevor's words shake him. He had to stay focused, had to find a way to end this once and for all. Summoning his last reserves of strength, Devin pushed himself up and faced Trevor head-on.

The warehouse echoed with the sounds of their struggle, the clashing of bodies and the heavy breaths of exertion. Devin fought with everything he had, but Trevor's relentless assault was overwhelming. Devin's vision began to blur, the edges of his consciousness slipping away. With a final, desperate effort, Devin swung his fist at Trevor, but his strength was fading. Trevor dodged the blow easily, then retaliated with a brutal strike that sent Devin crashing to the ground. Pain exploded through Devin's body, and darkness began to close in around him. Trevor stood over Devin, his eyes cold and merciless. "You can't stop me, Devin. Isabella will be mine." Devin's world began to fade, the sounds of the warehouse growing distant. His last thought before the darkness took him was of Isabella, her face a beacon of hope and love. He had to hold on for her. He couldn't let Trevor win.

Isabella paced anxiously outside the warehouse, her mind racing with worry. The officer had promised to help, but the wait was agonizing. Every second felt like an eternity, and the fear for Devin's safety gnawed at her heart. She glanced at the warehouse; her mind filled with the memories of the struggle she had witnessed. She couldn't bear the thought of Devin facing Trevor alone, but she knew she had to trust that help was on its way. Just as she was about to lose hope, the sound of sirens filled the air. A convoy of police cars pulled up, and officers quickly disembarked, their expressions serious and determined. Isabella's heart leapt with relief as she ran to meet them. "He's inside," she said urgently, pointing towards the warehouse. "Devin is fighting with Trevor. You have to help him." The lead officer nodded; his expression grim. "We'll take care of it. Stay here and stay safe." Isabella watched as the officers entered the warehouse, her heart pounding with a mixture of hope and fear. She prayed that Devin would be okay, that they would both make it out of this nightmare.

Inside the warehouse, the officers moved swiftly, their flashlights cutting through the darkness. They followed the sounds of the struggle, their weapons drawn and ready. As they rounded a corner, they spotted Trevor standing over Devin, his expression triumphant. "Freeze!" the lead officer shouted, his voice echoing through the warehouse. "Hands up!" Trevor's head snapped up; his eyes filled with rage. He hesitated for a moment, then turned and bolted towards the back of the warehouse. The officers gave chase, their footsteps pounding against the concrete floor. Devin lay on the ground, barely conscious. His vision was blurred, but he could see the figures moving around him, could hear the shouts and commands. He tried to move, but his body was weak, the pain overwhelming. One of the officers knelt beside him, his voice filled with concern. "Stay with us, Devin. Help is on the way." Devin's mind clung to the sound of the officer's voice, his thoughts a jumbled mess. He had to hold on. He had to make it through this for Isabella.

Trevor raced through the darkened corridors of the warehouse, his mind a whirlwind of anger and desperation. He had come so close to getting Isabella back, and now everything was falling apart. The sound of the officers' footsteps echoed behind him, and he knew he had to find a way out. He spotted a side door and sprinted towards it, his breath coming in ragged gasps. He burst through the door and into the night, the cool air hitting his face like a slap. He glanced around, searching for a place to hide, a way to escape. The warehouse was surrounded by a maze of alleyways and abandoned buildings. Trevor ducked into one of the alleys, his mind racing with plans and possibilities. He couldn't go back to jail. He couldn't let them take him. He had to find a way to disappear, to regroup and come back stronger. As he moved deeper into the shadows, he thought of Isabella. She had slipped through his fingers once again, but he wouldn't give up. He would find her. He would make her his. The thought fueled his determination, giving him the strength to keep going.

Isabella watched anxiously as the officers emerged from the warehouse, her heart pounding with a mixture of fear and hope. She spotted Devin being carried out on a stretcher, and her breath caught in her throat. She ran to his side, her eyes filled with tears. "Devin," she whispered, her voice trembling. "I'm here. You're going to be okay." Devin's eyes fluttered open, and he looked up at her, his expression filled with pain and relief. "Bella," he whispered, his voice weak. "You're safe." Isabella nodded, her tears falling freely. "Thanks to you. I love you, Devin. We'll get through this together." The paramedics loaded Devin into the ambulance, and Isabella climbed in beside him, holding his hand tightly. As the ambulance sped towards the hospital, she prayed for his recovery, for their future together.

But even as she clung to hope, a sense of dread lingered in the back of her mind. Trevor was still out there, somewhere in the shadows, plotting his next move. The battle was far from over, and the darkness that had haunted their lives was not yet vanquished. Trevor moved through the darkened streets, his mind a whirlwind of thoughts and plans. He had to find a place to hide, to regroup and plan his next move. He couldn't afford to be reckless. He had to be smart, to stay one step ahead of the authorities. He found an abandoned building and slipped inside, his eyes scanning the surroundings for any signs of danger. The building was empty, the air filled with the scent of decay and neglect. It was the perfect place to disappear, to plot his next move. As he settled into the shadows, his mind returned to Isabella. She had defied him, escaped his grasp, but he would not be disheartened. He would find her, no matter what it took. He would make her pay for every moment of defiance, for every time she had slipped through his fingers.

The thought filled him with a cold determination, a sense of purpose that drove him forward. He would bide his time, gather his strength, and strike when the moment was right. And when he did, Isabella would be his once and for all. For now, he would remain in the shadows, watching and waiting. The game was far from over, and he was determined to win. The darkness was his ally, his refuge, and he would use it to his advantage. As he settled into his hiding place, a sinister smile spread across his face. The battle had only just begun, and he was ready to do whatever it took to claim his prize. Isabella's days of freedom were numbered, and he would be the one to end them. The night grew darker, the air thick with an ominous sense of foreboding. Trevor's mind was a whirlwind of plans and schemes, each one more twisted than the last. He would not rest until Isabella was his, until he had reclaimed what he believed was rightfully his.

6

Uncertain Fate

The hospital's sterile white walls and the steady beeping of machines surrounded Isabella as she sat by Devin's bedside, holding his hand tightly. The faint glow of the bedside lamp cast shadows on Devin's pale face, highlighting the bruises and cuts from his confrontation with Trevor. Isabella's heart ached with worry and fear as she watched the rise and fall of his chest, each breath a reminder of his fragile state. The doctors had done their best, but the severity of Devin's injuries left his recovery uncertain. Isabella replayed the events of the last few hours in her mind, unable to shake the image of Trevor's menacing smile and the cold promise in his eyes. Devin had fought bravely to protect her, but now he lay unconscious, battling for his life. Isabella wiped away a tear, her mind filled with an uproar of emotions. The room felt suffocating, the weight of her anxiety pressing down on her. She glanced at the clock on the wall, its ticking a cruel reminder of the passing time. Every second felt like an eternity as she waited for any sign of improvement.

A soft knock on the door pulled her from her thoughts. She turned to see a nurse entering, her expression gentle but serious. "Mrs. Marcelli, is there anything I can get you? Something to eat or drink?" Isabella shook her head, her voice barely a whisper. "No, thank you. I'm fine." The nurse nodded and approached Devin's bed, checking his vitals and adjusting the IV drip. "He's stable for now," she said softly, offering a small smile of reassurance. "But it's going to be a long road to recovery." Isabella nodded, her grip on Devin's hand tightening. "Thank you," she whispered, her voice trembling with emotion. As the nurse left, Isabella leaned closer to Devin, her lips brushing against his forehead. "Please, Devin. You have to pull through. I need you. Sophia and Marco needs you."

Her mind drifted to their kids, who was staying with friends until Devin's condition stabilized. Isabella couldn't bear to bring Sophia and Marco to the hospital, to see their father in such a vulnerable state. The thought of their children's innocence being shattered by the harsh reality of their situation was too much to bear. Isabella closed her eyes, her thoughts swirling with memories of their life to-gether—the moments of joy and love, the challenges they had over-come, and the dreams they had for the future. She couldn't imagine a life without Devin by her side. He was her rock, her partner, her everything. As the hours passed, the uncertainty of Devin's fate gnawed at Isabella's soul. She felt a profound sense of helplessness, unable to do anything but wait and hope. The hospital's muted sounds—distant conversations, the hum of machinery, the occasional footsteps—blended into a haunting symphony of dread. Devin's doc-tor entered the room, his expression a mix of professionalism and concern. "Mrs. Marcelli," he began, his voice steady, "I wanted to give you an update on Devin's condition."

Isabella's heart raced as she looked up, her eyes searching the doc-tor's face for any hint of good news. "Yes, doctor?" "Devin sustained significant trauma during the altercation," the doctor explained. "We've managed to stabilize him, but he's still in critical condition. The next 24 to 48 hours will be crucial. His body needs time to heal, and we'll be monitoring him closely for any signs of improvement or complications." Isabella nodded; her throat tight with emotion. "Is there anything else I can do? Anything that might help him?" The doctor offered a sympathetic smile. "Just being here for him, talking to him, letting him know he's not alone—it can make a difference. Sometimes, the presence of a loved one can be a powerful motivator for recovery." Isabella's eyes filled with tears as she squeezed Devin's hand. "Thank you, doctor. I'll do everything I can."

As the doctor left, Isabella settled back into her chair, her mind racing with thoughts of their future. She refused to believe that this was the end. Devin was a fighter, and she had to believe that he would pull through. Devin floated in a sea of darkness, his mind a haze of pain and confusion. Memories of the confrontation with Trevor flickered like broken fragments, scattered with images of Isabella's face, her voice calling out to him. He felt himself drifting, the boundaries between consciousness and oblivion blurred.

In the depths of his mind, a sense of urgency began to stir. He couldn't leave Isabella alone. He couldn't let Trevor win. The thought of his family gave him strength, a glimmer of determination piercing through the fog of his injuries. He tried to move, to open his eyes, but his body felt heavy, unresponsive. The darkness seemed to press down on him, but he fought against it, his will to survive fueled by his love for Isabella, Sophia and Marco. Gradually, Devin became aware of a faint, distant sound—a voice, soft and familiar, calling his name. He focused on the sound, letting it guide him through the darkness. It was Isabella, her voice filled with love and desperation. "Devin, please. You have to come back to me. I need you. Sophia and Marco needs you. We can't do this without you." Her words resonated deep within him, igniting a spark of hope. He concentrated on her voice, willing himself to respond, to break free from the clutches of unconsciousness. The effort was exhausting, but he refused to give up.

Slowly, painfully, Devin's awareness began to sharpen. He could feel the pressure of Isabella's hand in his, the warmth of her touch grounding him in reality. He clung to that sensation, using it as an anchor to pull himself back. Isabella watched intently, her heart in her throat, as Devin's fingers twitched slightly in her grasp. It was a small movement, but it filled her with a surge of hope. She leaned closer, her voice trembling with emotion. "Devin? Can you hear me? Please, give me a sign." For a moment, there was no response, and Isabella's heart sank. But then, slowly, Devin's eyes fluttered open, his gaze unfocused but alive. Isabella's breath caught in her throat, tears streaming down her face. "Devin! Oh my God, Devin, you're awake!"

Devin blinked, his vision slowly clearing. He saw Isabella's tearstreaked face, her eyes filled with relief and love. He tried to speak, but his throat felt dry and raw. Isabella gently cupped his face, her touch tender and soothing. "Don't try to talk, just rest. You're going to be okay. We're going to get through this together." Devin managed a faint nod, the weight of his injuries pressing down on him. But the sight of Isabella, her unwavering presence, gave him the strength to keep fighting. He knew the road to recovery would be long and difficult, but he wasn't alone.

The days that followed were a blur of medical treatments and cautious optimism. Devin's condition remained critical, but each small sign of improvement was a beacon of hope for Isabella. She stayed by his side, her presence a constant source of comfort and encouragement. The hospital staff worked tirelessly to stabilize Devin's condition, administering treatments and monitoring his progress. Isabella's heart ached with gratitude for their dedication, but the uncertainty of Devin's fate continued to loom over her. One evening, as the sun set outside the hospital window, casting a warm glow over the room, Isabella sat by Devin's bedside, holding his hand. She spoke softly, her words a mix of love and determination.

"Devin, I know you're fighting with everything you have. And I want you to know that I'm right here with you, every step of the way. We're going to get through this. We're going to find a way to be happy again." Devin's eyes met hers, a flicker of emotion passing between them. He squeezed her hand weakly, his silent promise to keep fighting, to stay by her side. As the night deepened, Isabella's thoughts turned to Trevor. The threat he posed still lingered in the back of her mind, a constant reminder of the danger that had brought them to this point. She knew they couldn't let their guard down, even as they focused on Devin's recovery. But for now, in this moment, Isabella allowed herself to hope. She held Devin's hand tightly, finding strength in their love and the promise of a future together. The path ahead was uncertain, filled with challenges and unknowns, but they would face it together.

In the dark corners of his hideout, Trevor brooded, his mind a whirlwind of anger and frustration. News of Devin's condition had reached him, fueling his desire for revenge. He had come so close to reclaiming Isabella, and yet she had slipped through his grasp once again. But Trevor was nothing if not patient. He knew that his time would come, that he would find a way to strike again. The thought of Isabella filled his mind, a twisted obsession that drove him to plan and scheme. He would bide his time, gathering his strength and resources. The darkness was his ally, and he would use it to his advantage. Devin's recovery was a temporary setback, but it wouldn't discourage him.

As Trevor's thoughts churned with plans for the future, a sinister smile spread across his face. The game was far from over, and he was determined to win. The shadows would be his refuge, his weapon, and his victory. For now, he would watch and wait, letting the pieces fall into place. Isabella and Devin's love was a beacon of hope, but Trevor would be the one to extinguish it. The battle for Isabella's soul had only just begun, and Trevor was ready to fight with everything he had. The night stretched on, filled with a sense of impending doom. Trevor's eyes gleamed with a malevolent light; his mind focused on one thing: reclaiming Isabella. She was his obsession, his prize, and he would stop at nothing to claim her.

7

Trevor's Plan

The secluded cabin deep in the city was a perfect hiding place for Trevor. Far from prying eyes and the reach of law enforcement, it provided him the isolation he needed to devise his plan. The silence was comforting to Trevor, a sharp contrast to the chaos that had led him here. He had been on the run since escaping from the authorities, but now, he was ready to strike back.

Trevor sat at a makeshift desk, surrounded by maps, photographs, and notes. The faces of Devin and Isabella stared back at him from the photos, their lives laid bare through the surveillance he had carefully arranged. He had spent weeks studying their routines, understanding their habits, and identifying their vulnerabilities. Every detail was a piece of the puzzle, and Trevor was an expert at assembling it. His mind raced as he considered his options. The initial plan of psychological warfare had been successful, but it was only the beginning. He needed to take bolder steps to reclaim Isabella, to make her see that she belonged to him. The thought of her with Devin fueled his rage, but he knew that anger alone wouldn't bring her back. He needed to be strategic; to use the fear he had instilled to his advantage. Trevor began outlining his plan. The first step was to create a network of allies—individuals who could operate on the outside while he remained hidden. He had already contacted a few old acquaintances, men who owed him favors and shared his desire for power and control. They were willing to help for the right price, and Trevor had ensured they were well compensated.

He tapped a pen against the desk, considering his next move. Communication was key, and despite his isolation, Trevor had managed to secure a burner phone and a laptop with an encrypted connection. He used these tools to coordinate with his contacts, ensuring that every detail of his plan was executed flawlessly. Trevor's primary focus was on Isabella. He needed to break her spirit, to make her realize that she couldn't escape him. He would exploit her fears, her love for Devin, and her maternal instincts for Sophia and Marco. He would isolate her, make her feel vulnerable and alone. His contacts were already gathering information, learning every detail of Devin and Isabella's lives. They noted when Isabella dropped Sophia and Marco off at school, when Devin left for work, and the times they returned home. They tracked their movements, their interactions, and their moments of vulnerability. Every piece of information was fed back to Trevor, who analyzed it with meticulous care.

He started small, testing their reactions. A threatening note left on their car windshield; a shadowy figure seen outside their home at night. He wanted to instill a sense of paranoia, to make them question their own safety. The more they feared him, the more control he would have. Trevor's plan also involved exploiting Devin's weaknesses. He knew that Devin's protective instincts could be used against him. Trevor's contacts began to spread rumors, whispers of danger that would reach Devin's ears. He wanted Devin to feel the weight of responsibility, to drive a wedge between him and Isabella. If Devin was consumed by fear and doubt, he would be less capable of protecting his family. One of Trevor's most trusted allies was Alex, a former associate who had proven his loyalty time and again. Alex had a knack for gathering intel and staying under the radar, making him an invaluable asset. Trevor contacted Alex through an encrypted message, outlining the next phase of their plan.

"Alex, we need to step up our efforts. Increase surveillance on Isabella and Devin. I want to know every move they make. And start planting more seeds of doubt. Make them feel like they're always being watched." Alex replied swiftly, his loyalty unwavering. "Understood. I'll make sure they feel the pressure." With Alex handling the groundwork, Trevor could focus on the bigger picture. He envisioned a series of events that would erode their sense of security, pushing them to the brink of desperation. He would orchestrate a kidnapping, making it appear as though Isabella was in immediate danger. He would ensure that Devin was incapacitated, unable to protect her. In the chaos and confusion, Trevor would swoop in, presenting himself as her savior. Trevor's thoughts turned to Isabella. She was the key to his plan, the object of his obsession. He couldn't simply take her by force; he needed to break her spirit, to make her realize that she belonged to him. He would isolate her, make her feel vulnerable and alone.

One evening, as Trevor sat by the fire in the cabin, Alex called him on the burner phone. "We've gathered a lot of information. Devin is more paranoid than ever, and Isabella is starting to crack. What's the next move?" Trevor's lips curled into a sinister smile. "Good. Now we need to escalate. Arrange for an 'accident' to happen near their home. Nothing too serious, just enough to scare them. And keep the pressure on. I want them to feel like there's no escape." Alex agreed, and Trevor felt a surge of satisfaction. His plan was coming together. The psychological warfare was working, but he needed to be patient. The climax of his plan would be a final, devastating blow. He would stage the kidnapping in a way that left no doubt in Isabella's mind that she needed him.

As the days passed, Trevor's contacts continued their surveillance. They tracked Isabella and Devin's every move, noting the moments when they were most vulnerable. They arranged for small incidents—break-ins that left no trace, strange noises at night, unsettling phone calls. Each event chipped away at their sense of safety, heightening their anxiety. One night, as Isabella and Devin sat in their living room, the tension was palpable. The sense of unease that had settled over their lives was growing stronger, the invisible threat of Trevor's presence weighing heavily on their minds. Isabella glanced at Devin; her eyes filled with worry. "Devin, do you think it's him?" she asked, her voice barely above a whisper. Devin's jaw tightened; his eyes dark with anger. "It has to be. Who else would do this?" Isabella shuddered, wrapping her arms around herself. "What are we going to do?" "We need to stay vigilant," Devin replied, his tone resolute. "We'll increase security, change our routines. We can't let him win, Bella."

Isabella nodded, but the fear in her eyes was unmistakable. Trevor's plan was working; the seeds of doubt and fear were taking root. As the days passed, the sense of dread only grew stronger. The subtle threats continued, each one more unnerving than the last. Trevor celebrated in the chaos he was creating. He knew that the psychological warfare was just the beginning. He had more sinister plans in store, ways to push Devin and Isabella to their breaking point. He envisioned the moment when Isabella would finally realize that she had no choice but to come back to him, to seek his protection from the very dangers he had orchestrated. Trevor's mind buzzed with anticipation as he fine-tuned the details. He would use every resource at his disposal, every ally he had cultivated, to execute the plan flawlessly. The thought of reclaiming Isabella, of seeing the fear and desperation in her eyes, fueled his determination. Over the next few weeks, Trevor's plan began to take shape. His contacts increased their efforts, gathering more intel and orchestrating events that would heighten Devin and Isabella's paranoia. They arranged for a car accident near their home, leaving no physical evidence but instilling a deep sense of fear.

Trevor also began to exploit Devin's protective instincts. His contacts spread rumors of imminent danger, making Devin question his ability to protect his family. The psychological strain was evident, and Trevor knew it was only a matter of time before they reached their breaking point. One evening, as Isabella was locking up Bella's Haven, she noticed a figure lingering near the entrance. Her heart raced as she approached, ready to confront whoever it was. The figure stepped into the light, revealing Alex. "Are you Isabella?" She nodded, her guard up. "Who are you?" "My name is Alex. I have information about the people you're investigating. I used to work for one of them. I want to help, but I need protection." Isabella felt a mix of relief and suspicion. "Why should I trust you?" Alex's eyes pleaded with her. "I know you're skeptical, but I have proof. I was involved in their operations. I can give you names, locations, everything. But they'll kill me if they find out I'm talking to you."

Isabella considered his words, her mind racing. "Alright, come inside. We'll talk." Once inside, Alex began to recount his story. He described how he had become entangled with the powerful figures behind Trevor, providing names and details that matched the information Jamie had uncovered. He explained their operations, the illegal activities, and how they had managed to stay under the radar for so long. Isabella listened, her unease growing with each revelation. When Alex finished, she looked at him, her expression serious. "We can protect you, but we need everything you have. Documents, evidence, anything that can help us bring these people to justice." Alex nodded; his relief visible. "I have a stash of documents hidden. I can get them for you." Isabella and Devin decided to hide Alex in a safe house, ensuring his safety while they gathered more evidence. They contacted Jamie, updating him on the new development. Jamie agreed to help secure Alex's documents and analyze the information.

In the meantime, Trevor continued to orchestrate his plan from the shadows. He knew that his efforts were paying off, that Devin and Isabella were growing more desperate and fearful with each passing day. He enjoyed the thought of the final confrontation, the moment when he would reclaim Isabella and destroy Devin once and for all. As the night deepened, Trevor sat at his desk. His mind buzzed with anticipation; his thoughts consumed by the dark plans he had set in motion. The shadows were his allies, the darkness his refuge. And as the final pieces fell into place, Trevor knew that the moment of reckoning was near. The city around him was silent, but Trevor knew that his presence would soon be felt by Isabella and Devin.

8

A Desperate Race

The room was dimly lit, the only illumination coming from the flickering candle on the rickety wooden table. Trevor sat in a creaky chair; his eyes narrowed as he stared at a map spread out before him. His secluded hideout was in a remote, abandoned building on the outskirts of the city, a place he had meticulously chosen for its isolation. The shadows danced on the walls, creating an atmosphere of ominous intent. The night outside was thick with silence, broken only by the occasional car horn or siren. Trevor leaned back, running a hand through his messy hair as he contemplated his next move. He was furious, not just because he had been out smarted, but because Isabella had once again slipped through his fingers. The thought of her with Devin, living a life he felt should have been his, filled him with a seething rage.

His phone buzzed on the table, breaking the silence. Trevor picked it up, reading the message from Alex, his informant. "Everything is set. The documents are in place. It's time." A sinister smile crept across Trevor's face as he replied, "Good. Make sure nothing goes wrong. We need to execute this perfectly." Pocketing his phone, he turned back to the map. His plan was complicated, designed to lure Isabella and Devin into a trap they couldn't escape. He had spent months setting the stage, and now, the final act was about to begin. At the safe house, Isabella and Devin were in a state of heightened alert. The tension in the air was palpable, every noise outside making them jump. Isabella had barely slept, her mind troubled by the fear of what Trevor might do next. Devin, though equally exhausted, tried to remain strong for her. He kept a watchful eye on their surroundings, ready to defend his family at any moment. They had managed to secure Alex's documents, and Jamie was working tirelessly to uncover the truth behind Trevor's network. But time was running out.

Isabella sat by the window, staring out into the darkness. "Devin, what if we never get out of this? What if he always finds a way to come after us?" Devin walked over and wrapped his arms around her. "We will get through this, Bella. We have to stay strong and trust that Jamie will find what we need to end this nightmare." She leaned into him, drawing comfort from his presence. "I just want this to be over. I want us to have a normal life again." Devin kissed the top of her head. "We will. I promise." Their moment of solace was interrupted by a knock on the door. Devin tensed, reaching for the gun he had kept nearby. He approached the door cautiously, peering through the peephole. It was Jamie. Devin opened the door, letting Jamie in quickly. "What is it? Did you find something?"

Jamie nodded, his expression grave. "I did. But it's not good news. The documents Alex provided... they're a setup. Trevor planted them to lead us into a trap." Isabella's heart sank. "What do you mean?" Jamie placed a file on the table. "These documents outline a meeting location, supposedly where we can find more evidence against Trevor's associates. But it's a ruse. Trevor is planning to ambush you there." Devin's face darkened with anger. "So, what do we do? We can't just wait here and do nothing." Jamie nodded. "I agree. We need to turn the tables on Trevor. Use his own plan against him." They huddled together, devising a counter-strategy. They would go to the meeting location but with a tactical team in place, ready to capture Trevor. It was risky, but it was their best shot at ending this once and for all.

The night of the operation was pitch-black, clouds obscuring the moon and stars. The meeting location was an abandoned warehouse on the outskirts of town, a place that reeked of neglect and decay. Isabella, Devin, Jamie, and a team of armed officers approached cautiously, every step echoing ominously in the silent night. Trevor watched from a hidden vantage point, a satisfied grin spreading across his face as he saw Isabella and Devin arrive. Everything was going according to plan. He would make his move soon, and they would be helpless to stop him. Isabella's heart pounded in her chest as they entered the warehouse, her eyes darting around nervously. Devin was by her side, his grip on her hand reassuring. They moved deeper into the building, their footsteps the only sound in the crushing silence.

Suddenly, the lights flickered on, blinding them momentarily. Trevor stepped out from the shadows; his eyes gleaming with malice. "Welcome, Isabella. Devin. I've been expecting you." Devin stepped forward; his voice filled with anger. "This ends tonight, Trevor. We're taking you down." Trevor laughed, a cold, chilling sound. "You think you can stop me? You're out of your depth, Devin. I've planned this down to the last detail." He raised a hand, signaling to his hidden allies. Shots rang out, and chaos erupted. The tactical team engaged with Trevor's men, the sound of gunfire echoing through the warehouse. Devin pushed Isabella behind a stack of crates, shielding her with his body. "We have to get out of here, Bella," he shouted over the noise.

But Trevor wasn't done. He moved through the chaos with a predator's grace, his eyes locked on Isabella. She could feel his presence, a cold, menacing force that seemed to suffocate her. Devin turned to face Trevor, their eyes meeting in a moment of pure hatred. "This is your last chance, Trevor. Surrender, and maybe you'll live to see another day." Trevor sneered. "I'm not the one who's going to die here." He lunged at Devin, the two men clashing fiercely. Isabella watched in horror as they fought, her mind racing with fear and desperation. She knew she had to do something, but the chaos around her made it hard to think. Devin managed to land a punch, sending Trevor sprawling. He turned to Isabella. "Run, Bella! Get to safety!"

But before she could move, Trevor recovered, drawing a knife. He lunged at Devin, slashing wildly. Devin cried out in pain as the blade cut deep into his side. He fell to the ground, clutching his wound.

"Devin!" Isabella screamed, rushing to his side. Trevor loomed over them; his eyes filled with dark triumph. "You can't save him, Isabella. You can't save yourself." He moved to strike again, but a gunshot rang out, and Trevor stumbled back, clutching his shoulder. Jamie stood at the entrance; his gun trained on Trevor. "It's over, Trevor. Drop the knife." Trevor hesitated, then turned and fled into the night. Jamie rushed to Devin and Isabella; his face grim. "We need to get him to a hospital, now." The ride to the hospital was a blur of flashing lights and sirens. Isabella held Devin's hand tightly, praying silently for his survival. He was unconscious, his face pale from blood loss. Jamie drove with grim determination, the tension in the car palpable.

They arrived at the hospital, and Devin was whisked away by the medical team. Isabella and Jamie were left in the waiting room, the minutes dragging by like hours. The ominous feeling that had plagued them for so long seemed to hang in the air, thick and suffocating. Isabella couldn't sit still. She paced the room, her mind filled with fear and uncertainty. Jamie watched her, his expression filled with concern. "He'll make it, Isabella. Devin's strong." She nodded, but her heart was heavy with dread. "I just... I can't lose him, Jamie. Not after everything we've been through." Jamie stood and placed a reassuring hand on her shoulder. "We'll get through this. Together." Meanwhile, Trevor staggered through the city, his shoulder throbbing with pain. He had lost this battle, but the war was far from over. His mind raced with thoughts of revenge, of finishing what he had started.

He reached his hideout, collapsing onto the floor. He needed medical attention, but there was no one he could trust. He would have to patch himself up and plan his next move carefully. Devin and Isabella had proven to be formidable opponents, but Trevor was nothing if not relentless. He pulled out a first aid kit, gritting his teeth against the pain as he cleaned and bandaged his wound. His mind buzzed with dark thoughts, his obsession with Isabella driving him forward. He would find a way to get her back, no matter the cost. As he sat in the dim light of the hideout, the shadows seemed to close in around him, mirroring the darkness in his soul. He knew he couldn't afford any more mistakes. His next move had to be flawless, calculated to strike fear into the hearts of Isabella and Devin.

9

Unrelenting Shadows

The sterile smell of the hospital clung to Isabella as she sat in the waiting room, her fingers intertwined tightly with Devin's, even though he was unconscious and hooked up to a multitude of machines. Every beep and hum sent a jolt of fear through her, a constant reminder of the precariousness of Devin's condition. Jamie sat across from her, his face etched with concern. Hours had passed since they brought Devin in, and the doctors had been working tirelessly to stabilize him. Isabella's mind raced with fear and uncertainty, the sinister events of the past few days hanging over her like a dark cloud. The sight of Devin, so strong and unwavering, now so vulnerable, tore at her heart.

Jamie finally broke the silence, his voice soft but steady. "Isabella, you need to rest. You haven't slept in days." She shook her head, her eyes never leaving Devin's face. "I can't, Jamie. What if something happens? What if he...?" Jamie leaned forward, placing a comforting hand on her shoulder. "He's a fighter, Isabella. Devin's strong. He'll pull through this." Isabella's eyes filled with tears. "But what if he doesn't? What if Trevor takes everything from me? I can't lose him, Jamie. I just can't." Jamie sighed, his own heart heavy with worry. "We won't let that happen. We'll find Trevor, and we'll make sure he can't hurt anyone ever again." The door to the waiting room opened, and a doctor stepped in, her expression serious. "Isabella?" Isabella stood, her heart in her throat. "Yes, that's me. How is he?" The doctor gave her a reassuring smile. "Devin's condition is stable. He lost a lot of blood, but we were able to stop the bleeding and repair the damage. He's in recovery now, but it will be a while before he's fully out of the woods."

Relief washed over Isabella, her legs almost giving way beneath her. Jamie caught her, helping her back into her seat. "Thank you," she whispered to the doctor. The doctor nodded. "He'll need to stay here for a while to recover. And you should get some rest too. He'll need you to be strong for him." Isabella nodded, but she knew sleep would be difficult. Her mind was still racing, the shadow of Trevor's threat looming large. As the doctor left, Jamie sat down beside her, his expression thoughtful. "Isabella, we need to talk," he said gently. "About Devin, and about what we do next." Isabella looked at him, her eyes red-rimmed from lack of sleep and tears. "What do you mean, Jamie?" Jamie took a deep breath. "I know you're scared. I am too. But we can't let fear paralyze us. Trevor is still out there, and he's not going to stop until he gets what he wants. We need to be proactive. We need to protect Devin and take the fight to Trevor."

Isabella nodded slowly, the reality of their situation sinking in. "You're right. But how do we do that? How do we fight someone like Trevor?" Jamie leaned back, his mind working through the possibilities. "We need to find him first. And for that, we need help. More resources, more people who know how to track someone like him. I've already reached out to some contacts in law enforcement and private security. We need to be ready for anything." Isabella swallowed hard, the size of their task weighing heavily on her. "And what about Devin? What if he doesn't recover fully?" Jamie met her gaze, his eyes filled with determination. "Then we'll fight for him. We'll do whatever it takes to make sure he's safe. But right now, we need to focus on the immediate threat. Trevor's plan, whatever it is, we need to uncover it and stop him." Isabella nodded, her resolve strengthening. "You're right, Jamie. We can't let him win. Not again."

As the night wore on, Jamie and Isabella continued to plan, their conversation punctuated by the occasional beep of the monitors in Devin's room. They discussed every possible scenario, every way they could protect themselves and their loved ones. It was a daunting task, but they knew they couldn't afford to fail. Meanwhile, in his hideout, Trevor was carefully preparing for his next move. The pain in his shoulder was a constant reminder of his failure, but it only fueled his determination. He had spent the past few days studying the information Alex had provided, crafting a plan that would finally bring Isabella back to him. Trevor's hideout was a huge abandoned factory on the outskirts of the city. The walls were covered in maps and photos, all part of his elaborate scheme. He paced the room, his mind racing with thoughts of revenge and obsession. He had always been meticulous in his planning, and this time was no different. He knew every detail of Isabella and Devin's lives, every move they made. His eyes fell on a photo of Isabella, her face filled with joy and love. It was a photo taken during happier times, before everything had gone wrong.

Trevor's face twisted with anger as he looked at the photo. "You should have been mine, Isabella. We were meant to be together." He turned his attention to the map on the wall, a detailed layout of the hospital where Devin was recovering. He had been watching them closely, waiting for the perfect moment to strike. He knew he couldn't afford any more mistakes. Trevor's plan was simple yet effective. He would use the hospital's vulnerabilities to his advantage, slipping in unnoticed and taking Isabella while Devin was still incapacitated. It was risky, but he thrived on risk. It was what made him who he was. He gathered his supplies, checking and rechecking everything. He couldn't afford to leave anything to chance. The darkness outside seemed to echo his intentions, the city closing in around him like a shroud. He relished the feeling, the thrill of the hunt.

As he prepared to leave, Trevor's mind wandered back to the day he had first met Isabella. She had been so full of life, so vibrant. He had been captivated by her, and he had promised himself that he would do whatever it took to make her his. But things had not gone as planned. She had chosen Devin, and Trevor's obsession had turned to anger and resentment. Now, standing in the shadows of his hideout, Trevor felt a twisted sense of satisfaction. He was close to achieving his goal, and nothing would stand in his way. He would have Isabella, and he would make sure Devin paid for taking her from him. With one last look at the map, Trevor slipped out of the hideout, the darkness swallowing him whole. The night was his ally, the shadows his weapon. He moved with the precision of a predator, every step bringing him closer to his prey.

Back at the hospital, Isabella finally allowed herself to rest, her body giving in to the exhaustion that had been building for days. She sat beside Devin's bed, her head resting on the edge of the mattress. The soft beeping of the monitors was a strange comfort, a reminder that he was still with her. Jamie watched over them, his mind racing with plans and contingencies. He knew they couldn't afford to let their guard down, not with Trevor still out there. He had set up a security detail around the hospital, but the sense of unease never left him. In the early hours of the morning, Isabella stirred, her eyes fluttering open. She looked at Devin, his face peaceful in sleep, and felt a surge of love and determination. She wouldn't let Trevor win. She would fight for her family, no matter the cost. Jamie walked over, offering her a cup of coffee. "How are you holding up?" Isabella took the cup, grateful for the warmth. "As well as can be expected. I'm just... scared, Jamie. What if Trevor finds us again?"

Jamie sat beside her; his expression serious. "We're doing everything we can to keep you safe. But we need to be ready for anything. I've been working on a plan to track Trevor down. We have to find him before he finds us." Isabella nodded, her resolve hardening. "What do we need to do?" Jamie outlined his plan, detailing the steps they would take to locate Trevor. They would use every resource available, every contact they had, to track him down. It was a daunting task, but they had no choice. As the sun began to rise, casting a pale light over the hospital, Isabella felt a glimmer of hope. They were in for a long and difficult battle, but she knew they had to fight. For Devin, for their family, for their future. The day stretched on, filled with preparations and planning. Jamie coordinated with his contacts, setting everything in motion. Isabella stayed by Devin's side, her heart aching with love and fear. She knew the road ahead would be filled with danger, but she was ready to face it.

As night fell once again, the sense of unease returned, the shadows lengthening and closing in around them. Isabella and Jamie knew they were racing against time, the threat of Trevor's return hanging over them like a dark cloud. But despite the fear, despite the uncertainty, they held on to hope. They had each other, and they had a plan. And with that, they faced the darkness, ready to fight for their lives and their future. In the depths of the night, as Trevor moved through the streets, the ominous feeling that had plagued them all grew stronger. The final confrontation was drawing closer, and they all knew it. The shadows were closing in, but Isabella and Jamie were determined to fight back, to protect what mattered most. The battle was far from over, and as the night stretched on, they prepared for the storm that was about to come.

10

Into the Shadows

The hospital's sterile environment felt more like a prison than a place of healing. The low hum of machines and the soft beeps that monitored Devin's vital signs created an unsettling rhythm that echoed through the corridors. Isabella stood by the window in Devin's room, staring out at the dark, stormy night. The rain lashed against the glass, mirroring the turmoil within her. Devin's condition had stabilized, but the doctors remained cautious. He was still unconscious, fighting a battle within himself. Isabella's heart ached as she watched him, helpless to do anything but wait. Jamie had just left, promising to return with more information about Trevor's whereabouts. The constant fear of Trevor's next move loomed over them like a dark cloud.

Isabella turned back to Devin, reaching out to gently brush a strand of hair from his forehead. "Please, Devin," she whispered, her voice trembling. "Come back to me." Her thoughts were interrupted by the sound of the door opening. She turned to see a nurse entering the room, carrying a tray of medical supplies. The nurse offered a reassuring smile. "Mrs. Marcelli, would you like some time to rest? We can watch over him for a while." Isabella shook her head. "Thank you, but I want to stay with him." The nurse nodded, understanding. "If you need anything, just let us know." As the nurse left, Isabella resumed her vigil. The hours passed slowly, each minute stretching into an eternity. The storm outside showed no signs of subsiding, the relentless rain adding to the sense of anxiety. Isabella felt the weight of exhaustion bearing down on her, but she refused to leave Devin's side. Suddenly, a soft knock on the door broke the silence. Jamie stepped in; his face etched with worry. "Isabella, we need to talk." She looked up, her eyes filled with anxiety. "Did you find him?"

Jamie nodded, but his expression was grim. "Yes, but it's complicated. Trevor is hiding out in an abandoned factory on the outskirts of the city. It's heavily guarded, and he's not alone. He has a few men with him, probably to keep watch and protect him." Isabella's heart sank. "What are we going to do?" Jamie sat down beside her; his tone serious. "We need to be smart about this. We can't just storm in there. It would be too dangerous. We need a plan to lure him out, to catch him off guard." Isabella nodded, her mind racing. "What do you suggest?" Jamie took a deep breath. "We set a trap. We make him think he's won, that he can get to you. But we'll be ready for him. We have to make sure he doesn't see it coming." Isabella's stomach churned at the thought of being used as bait, but she knew it was their best chance. "I'll do it. Whatever it takes to stop him." Jamie placed a reassuring hand on her shoulder. "We'll make sure you're safe, Isabella. We'll have backup, and we'll be ready for anything."

The plan was set in motion quickly. Jamie coordinated with the authorities, setting up surveillance around Trevor's hideout and preparing for the ambush. Isabella tried to focus on the task at hand, but her thoughts kept drifting back to Devin. She needed him to wake up, to be by her side as they faced this new threat. As night fell again, the hospital seemed to grow colder. Isabella sat by Devin's bedside; her fingers entwined with his. She whispered softly to him, hoping that her voice would reach him, wherever he was. Meanwhile, Trevor sat at the makeshift table in the factory, staring at a map spread out on the table. The flickering candlelight cast eerie shadows on the walls, adding to the ominous atmosphere. His men were stationed outside, keeping watch for any signs of intrusion. Trevor's mind was consumed with thoughts of Isabella. He had come so close to having her, and he would not be denied again.

He traced a path on the map with his finger, planning his next move. He knew he had to be careful, to avoid falling into any traps. But his obsession with Isabella clouded his judgment, making him more reckless. He glanced at a photograph of her, a twisted smile forming on his lips. "Soon," he muttered to himself. "Soon you'll be mine again." He gathered his men inside, briefing them on his plan. They would move under the cover of darkness, using the storm to their advantage. He would make his way to the hospital, taking Isabella by surprise. He had no intention of failing this time. Back at the hospital, Isabella felt a sense of unease growing stronger. The storm outside had intensified, the wind howling like a mournful wail. She looked at Devin, willing him to wake up, to give her strength. She glanced at the clock, noting the time. Jamie and the team would be in position soon.

As if sensing her thoughts, Devin stirred slightly, a faint groan escaping his lips. Isabella's heart leaped with hope. "Devin? Can you hear me?" His eyes fluttered open, and for a moment, he seemed disoriented. But as his gaze focused on Isabella, a flicker of recognition appeared. "Bella..." Tears of relief filled her eyes. "I'm here, Devin. You're going to be okay." He tried to sit up, but winced in pain. Isabella gently pushed him back down. "Don't try to move. You need to rest." Devin's voice was weak but determined. "What about Trevor? Is he still out there?" Isabella nodded; her expression serious. "Yes, but Jamie and the team are setting a trap. We're going to catch him." Devin's eyes hardened with resolve. "Be careful, Bella. He's dangerous."

"I will," she promised. "You just focus on getting better." Trevor moved through the streets with his men, the rain drenching them but providing cover for their approach. They reached the edge of the hospital grounds, pausing to assess the situation. Trevor's heart raced with anticipation. He could almost taste victory. He signaled for his men to spread out, creating a perimeter. He would go in alone, slipping through the shadows to reach Isabella. He moved with the stealth of a predator; his eyes fixed on his target. Inside the hospital, Jamie and his team were in position, watching the monitors and waiting for the signal. Isabella stood by Devin's bed, her nerves on edge. She knew the plan, but the uncertainty gnawed at her. Suddenly, Jamie's voice came through the earpiece. "He's here. Stay alert." Isabella's heart pounded as she looked around the dimly lit room. The storm outside seemed to intensify, the wind rattling the windows. She moved closer to Devin, her hand resting on the edge of the bed. The door creaked open slowly, and Trevor stepped inside, his eyes gleaming with malevolent intent. He saw Isabella and smiled; his twisted sense of triumph evident. "Isabella," he said softly, taking a step closer. "I've come to take you back."

Isabella's breath caught in her throat, but she stood her ground. "You won't win, Trevor. We're ready for you." Trevor's smile widened. "We'll see about that." Just as he reached out to grab her, Jamie and the team burst into the room, weapons drawn. Trevor's men outside were quickly subdued, the element of surprise working in their favor. Trevor snarled in anger, realizing he had been outmaneuvered. He lunged at Isabella, but Jamie intercepted him, knocking him to the ground. The struggle was intense, but Jamie's training and determination prevailed. Trevor was finally restrained, his plans foiled. As the authorities took Trevor away, Isabella felt a wave of relief wash over her. She turned to Devin, who had watched the entire scene unfold with a mixture of worry and pride. "You did it, Bella," Devin said weakly, a small smile forming on his lips.

"We did it," she corrected, leaning down to kiss his forehead. "Together." The threat of Trevor was finally over, but the shadows of their past would linger. Isabella knew they would face more challenges, but with Devin by her side, she felt ready to confront anything. As the storm outside began to subside, a sense of calm settled over the hospital. The future was still uncertain, but their love and determination had proven stronger than the darkness that had threatened to consume them. Together, they would face whatever came next, their bond unbreakable and their hearts filled with hope. The journey ahead would be long and difficult, but they were ready to face it, hand in hand, heart to heart. The shadows of fate had been cast, but they would emerge stronger, their love guiding them through the darkness.

11

Shadows of Recovery

The sun rose over the hospital, casting a pale, hesitant light through the windows of Devin's room. The storm had passed, but an eerie stillness lingered, as if the world held its breath in the wake of Trevor's capture. Isabella sat by Devin's bedside, her fingers entwined with his, as she watched the steady rise and fall of his chest. He was conscious now, but the road to recovery was long and uncertain. Isabella glanced at the clock, noting that it was almost time for Devin's discharge. The doctors had assured her that he was well enough to continue his recovery at home, but the fear of another attack from Trevor still gnawed at her. She took a deep breath, trying to steady her nerves.

Devin's eyes fluttered open, and he smiled weakly at her. "Morning, Bella." She returned his smile, though her eyes betrayed her worry. "Morning, Devin. How are you feeling?" "Better, now that I'm going home," he replied, his voice still weak but filled with determination. A nurse entered the room, carrying a clipboard. "Good morning, Mr. Marcelli. Are you ready to go home?" Devin nodded. "More than ready." The nurse smiled warmly. "I'll get everything set up for your discharge. Mrs. Marcelli, if you could fill out these forms, we'll have you on your way in no time." As Isabella completed the paperwork, her mind raced with thoughts of their return home. They had taken steps to ensure their safety, but the memory of Trevor's malevolent presence still haunted her. She knew they had to remain vigilant, even in the sanctuary of their home.

The drive home was quiet, the tension visible. Isabella stole glances at Devin, who seemed lost in thought. Their daughter, Sophia, and their son, Marco, were with Isabella's sister, giving them time to settle back in without overwhelming Devin. When they arrived at their house, Isabella helped Devin inside, guiding him to the couch in the living room. The house was eerily silent, the shadows cast by the morning sun creating an ominous atmosphere. "Do you need anything, Devin?" Isabella asked, her voice soft. He shook his head. "Just you, Bella. Just you." She sat beside him, her heart aching at the sight of his frailty. "We'll get through this, Devin. Together."

He reached for her hand, squeezing it gently. "I know we will." The days that followed were a blur of doctors' visits, physical therapy sessions, and moments of quiet reflection. Devin's recovery was slow, each step forward met with new challenges. Isabella remained by his side, her love and determination unwavering. One afternoon, as Devin rested in bed, Isabella received a call from Jamie. His voice was tense. "Isabella, we need to talk. Can you meet me at Bella's Haven?" Isabella's heart skipped a beat. "Is everything okay?" "Just come. We need to discuss something important." She glanced at Devin, who was dozing peacefully, then made a decision. "I'll be there soon." When she arrived at Bella's Haven, Jamie was waiting for her in the office. His expression was grim. "We have a problem." Isabella felt a chill run down her spine. "What is it?" "Trevor's capture wasn't as clean-cut as we thought. Some of his associates are still out there, and they're not happy about his arrest. They've been asking questions, looking for information about you and Devin."

Isabella's mind raced. "What do we do?" Jamie leaned forward; his eyes intense. "We need to tighten security. I've already spoken to the authorities, and they're increasing patrols around your house. But we need to be prepared for anything." Isabella nodded, her resolve hardening. "We'll do whatever it takes to protect our family." Back at home, Isabella shared the news with Devin. His reaction was a mix of anger and determination. "We can't let them win, Bella. We have to stay strong." "We will," she assured him. "We'll get through this, just like we have with everything else." Their resolve was put to the test in the weeks that followed. The increased security provided some comfort, but the fear of another attack lingered. Devin's recovery continued, each small victory a testament to his strength and resilience.

One evening, as the family gathered in the living room, Sophia climbed onto Devin's lap, her eyes filled with curiosity. "Daddy, are you feeling better?" Devin smiled, ruffling her hair. "I'm getting there, sweetheart. Thanks to you and your mommy." Marco toddled over, holding out a toy for Devin. "Play, Daddy?" Devin chuckled, taking the toy from his son. "Of course, buddy. Let's play."

Isabella watched them, her heart swelling with love and gratitude. Despite the darkness that had threatened to consume them, moments like these reminded her of the light that still existed in their lives. Late one night, as Isabella lay in bed beside Devin, she couldn't shake the feeling of unease. The house was quiet, but the shadows seemed to whisper of danger. She turned to Devin, who was already looking at her. "Can't sleep?" he asked softly. She shook her head. "I keep thinking about Trevor. Even with him gone, it feels like he's still here, lurking in the shadows." Devin reached out, pulling her close. "We'll be okay, Bella. We have each other, and we have the kids. That's what matters." "I know," she whispered, resting her head on his chest. "But it's hard to let go of the fear." "We'll take it one day at a time," Devin said gently. "And we'll face whatever comes together."

The following morning, as the sun began to rise, Isabella felt a renewed sense of determination. She had faced darkness before, and she had emerged stronger. She would do the same now, for Devin, for their children, and for herself. Jamie arrived later that day, bringing updates on the situation. "The authorities are keeping a close watch on Trevor's associates. We're doing everything we can to ensure your safety." Isabella nodded. "Thank you, Jamie. We appreciate everything you're doing." "We're in this together," Jamie replied. "We'll get through it." As the weeks turned into months, the fear that had once gripped their lives began to loosen its hold. Devin's strength returned, his recovery progressing steadily. The children brought joy and laughter into their home, their innocence a balm for the wounds that had been inflicted.

One evening, as the family gathered for dinner, Isabella felt a sense of peace she hadn't experienced in a long time. They had faced the darkness and had come out stronger on the other side. There were still challenges ahead, but they were ready to face them together. After dinner, as the children played in the living room, Isabella and Devin sat on the porch, watching the stars. The night was calm, the air filled with the soft sounds of nature. Devin took Isabella's hand, his grip strong and reassuring. "We've been through a lot, Bella. But we've made it." She smiled, leaning into him. "We have. And we'll keep going, no matter what." As they sat together, the future stretched out before them, filled with both uncertainty and hope. The shadows that had once threatened to consume them had been pushed back, replaced by the light of their love and determination.

For now, they held onto the present, cherishing each moment of peace and happiness. They knew that the darkness could return, but they were ready to face it, together. Their love had proven stronger than any shadow, and it would continue to guide them through whatever challenges lay ahead. The future was theirs to shape, and with their love as their guiding light, they knew they could overcome anything. As the stars twinkled overhead, Isabella felt a deep sense of gratitude. They had faced the darkness and emerged stronger; their love unbreakable. And as they looked to the future, they knew that, no matter what, they would face it together, with hope and determination guiding their way.

12

The Shadows Return

The weeks following Devin's return home were filled with moments of joy and healing, but an undercurrent of dread lingered. Isabella couldn't shake the feeling that they were living on borrowed time. The security measures they had put in place provided some comfort, but the threat of Trevor's associates loomed like a dark cloud over their happiness. One late evening, Isabella stood on the porch, watching the stars as she often did when she couldn't sleep. The house was quiet, the soft sounds of Sophia and Marco's gentle breathing drifting through the open window. Devin was asleep inside, his recovery progressing well, but Isabella's mind refused to rest.

She wrapped her arms around herself, the cool night air sending a shiver down her spine. The events of the past months had taken their toll, and though they had emerged stronger, the fear of what could happen next gnawed at her. She was about to head back inside when her phone buzzed in her pocket. Isabella glanced at the screen, her heart skipping a beat. It was an unknown number. A sense of déjà vu washed over her as she answered the call. "Hello?" There was a brief silence on the other end, followed by a voice that sent a chill down her spine. "Isabella, it's time you knew the truth." Her grip tightened on the phone. "Who is this?" The voice was calm, almost too calm. "I'm someone who has been watching from the shadows. I know about Trevor, and I know about the man who has been pulling the strings all along." Isabella's heart raced. "What do you want?" "It's not about what I want, Isabella. It's about what you need to know. The man you're looking for is powerful, and he's closer than you think. If you want to protect your family, you need to act now."

The call disconnected, leaving Isabella with a sense of dread and urgency. She stood there, her mind racing, trying to piece together the cryptic message. Who was this man, and how could she protect her family from him? She went inside, her mind still reeling. Devin stirred as she entered the bedroom, his eyes opening to find her standing in the doorway, pale and shaken. "Bella, what's wrong?" Isabella took a deep breath, trying to steady herself. "I got another call. They said the man pulling the strings is closer than we think. We need to be careful, Devin." Devin sat up; his expression serious. "Did they give any more information?" She shook her head. "No, just that we need to act now to protect our family." Devin's jaw tightened. "We'll figure this out, Bella. We'll protect our family."

The next few days were tense, filled with a sense of anxiety. Isabella and Devin increased their security measures, installing additional locks and surveillance cameras. Jamie was informed of the latest development, and he worked tirelessly to track down the source of the call. One night, as the family sat down for dinner, a sense of normalcy settled over them. Laughter filled the air as Sophia and Marco recounted their day, their innocent joy a stark contrast to the darkness that loomed over them. Isabella forced herself to smile, trying to push the fear to the back of her mind. After dinner, as they put the children to bed, Isabella felt a sense of unease creeping back. She and Devin checked the locks and security system one last time before heading to bed. Isabella lay awake, her mind racing with thoughts of the mysterious caller and the unknown threat. Suddenly, a loud crash echoed through the house, shattering the silence. Isabella sat up, her heart pounding. Devin was already on his feet, grabbing the baseball bat he kept by the bed. "Stay here with the kids," he whispered, his eyes filled with determination.

Isabella nodded, her fear for their safety overwhelming. She quickly moved to the children's room, her mind racing. She could hear the sounds of footsteps and muffled voices downstairs. Her hands shook as she held Sophia and Marco close, trying to keep them calm. Devin moved cautiously through the house, his grip on the bat tightening with each step. He reached the living room, finding the front door wide open, the lock broken. Shadows moved in the darkness, and he could hear the intruders whispering to each other. He took a deep breath, stepping into the room. "Who's there?" he called out, his voice steady despite the fear gripping him. The intruders froze, their eyes glinting in the dim light. "We're here for the girl," one of them sneered, stepping forward. "You can't protect her forever." Devin's grip on the bat tightened. "Get out of my house."

The intruder laughed, a cold, menacing sound. "You think you can stop us? We're just the beginning." Devin lunged forward, swinging the bat with all his strength. The intruder dodged, pulling out a knife. Devin's heart raced as he fought, the sound of the struggle echoing through the house. Upstairs, Isabella listened, her fear for Devin growing with each passing second. She held the children close, whispering reassurances to them. The sounds of the fight grew louder, and then there was silence. Isabella's heart pounded in her chest as she waited, straining to hear any sign of Devin. The silence was deafening, each second feeling like an eternity. Finally, she heard footsteps on the stairs, and Devin appeared in the doorway, breathing heavily but unharmed. "They're gone," he said, his voice shaking with adrenaline. "But they'll be back. We need to be ready." Isabella nodded; her relief tempered by the knowledge that the danger was far from over. They couldn't let their guard down, not for a moment. The shadows that had once seemed distant were now closing in, and they had to be prepared for whatever came next.

The following days were a blur of preparations and heightened vigilance. Devin and Isabella worked tirelessly to fortify their home, their fear driving them to take every possible precaution. Jamie provided additional support, arranging for increased patrols and monitoring the situation closely. One evening, as Isabella sat in the living room, her phone buzzed with a message from Jamie. "I have some information. We need to meet." Isabella glanced at Devin, who was sitting nearby. "Jamie has news. I'm going to meet him." Devin nodded. "Be careful, Bella." She left the house, her mind racing with thoughts of what Jamie might have discovered. When she arrived at Bella's Haven, Jamie was waiting for her in the office, his expression grim. "I've been digging deeper," he said, handing her a folder. "The man behind this, the one pulling the strings, is someone we've crossed paths with before. His name is Victor Kane."

Isabella's heart skipped a beat. "Victor Kane? But he disappeared years ago." Jamie nodded. "He went underground, but he's been building his power in the shadows. He's dangerous, Bella. More dangerous than Trevor." Isabella's mind raced as she processed the information. "What do we do?" Jamie leaned forward; his eyes intense. "We need to gather more evidence. We can't take him down without it. But you need to be careful. Victor will stop at nothing to get what he wants." Isabella nodded, her resolve hardening. "We'll do whatever it takes." Back at home, Isabella shared the news with Devin. His reaction was a mix of anger and determination. "Victor Kane... I thought we'd seen the last of him." "Apparently not," Isabella said. "We need to stay vigilant. We can't let him win." Their resolve was put to the test that night. As the family settled into bed, the sense of anxiety grew. Isabella lay awake, her mind racing with thoughts of Victor and his plans. The shadows outside seemed to move with a life of their own, and every creak of the house set her on edge.

13

The Trap Tightens

The aftermath of the home invasion left Isabella and Devin on edge, their home feeling more like a fortress under siege than a sanctuary. They took turns sleeping, always on high alert, knowing that their enemies were closing in. Despite the heightened security, Isabella couldn't shake the feeling that they were still vulnerable.

The call from Jamie had given them a name—Victor Kane. A man who had vanished years ago, only to resurface as the mastermind behind their current nightmare. Isabella and Devin spent countless hours scanning over files, trying to piece together any information that could give them an edge. But Victor Kane was a ghost, leaving behind only whispers of his influence. One morning, Isabella decided to leave the house to gather supplies for Bella's Haven. She needed to feel useful, to do something that made her feel normal. Devin insisted on accompanying her, but Isabella, sensing his exhaustion, convinced him to stay home with the children. "I'll be quick," she promised, giving him a reassuring smile. "I'll take every precaution. You need to rest." Devin reluctantly agreed, his protective instincts conflicting with his understanding of her need for some semblance of normalcy. "Just be careful, Bella. And call me if anything feels off."

Isabella kissed him goodbye and headed out, her heart heavy with a mixture of dread and determination. She made her way through the city, her eyes constantly scanning her surroundings. Every shadow seemed threatening, every unfamiliar face a potential enemy. As she finished loading supplies into her car, she felt a prickling sensation on the back of her neck. Before she could react, a van screeched to a halt beside her, and masked men jumped out, grabbing her roughly. She struggled, but they were too strong. A cloth was pressed over her mouth, and the world faded into darkness. When Isabella awoke, her head was pounding. She was lying on a cold, hard floor, her wrists and ankles bound. The room was dimly lit, the air thick with the smell of damp and decay. She struggled to sit up, her heart pounding as she took in her surroundings. She was in an abandoned factory, its vast, empty spaces echoing with an eerie silence.

Fear clawed at her, but she forced herself to stay calm. She had to think, had to find a way out. The sound of footsteps echoed through the factory, and she tensed, her heart racing. The door creaked open, and two men entered, their expressions cold and detached. "Get up," one of them ordered, grabbing her arm and pulling her to her feet. She stumbled, but they held her up, dragging her out of the room and down a long, dark hallway. They brought her to a large, open space where a figure stood waiting in the shadows. As they approached, the figure stepped into the light, and Isabella's blood ran cold. It was Trevor. "Well, well," Trevor said, his voice dripping with malice. "Look who we have here." Isabella glared at him, refusing to show fear. "What do you want, Trevor?" He smirked, stepping closer. "I want what's mine, Bella. And that includes you."

"You'll never get away with this," she spat. "Devin will find me." Trevor laughed, a cruel, mocking sound. "Devin is the least of your worries. There are bigger players in this game now." At that moment, another figure stepped out of the shadows. Victor Kane. His presence was commanding, his expression one of cold calculation. He looked at Isabella with a mixture of curiosity and disdain. "So, you're the famous Isabella," Victor said, his voice smooth and menacing. "I've heard a lot about you." Isabella felt a chill run down her spine. "Let me go." Victor smiled, a predatory gleam in his eyes. "I don't think so. You see, you've become a very valuable piece in this game. And I intend to use you to my advantage."

He stepped closer, his demeanor menacing. "I've spent years building my power, and I won't let anyone stand in my way. Not you, not your husband, not anyone." Isabella's fear turned to anger. "You're a coward, hiding behind your power and your thugs. You'll never win." Victor's smile faded, replaced by a look of cold fury. He grabbed her by the chin, forcing her to look into his eyes. "You don't understand the gravity of your situation, Isabella. I don't play games. I win. And you, my dear, are going to help me do just that." He released her roughly, and she stumbled back, her heart pounding with fear and anger. "What are you going to do to me?" Victor turned to Trevor, his expression cold and calculating. "Keep her here. Make sure she understands that any attempt to escape will be met with severe consequences."

Trevor nodded, a twisted smile on his face. "Don't worry, I'll make sure she knows her place." Victor looked back at Isabella; his eyes filled with menace. "I'll be back to check on you, Isabella. And you'd better hope you're cooperative. Otherwise, things will get very unpleasant for you and your family." With that, he turned and left, his footsteps echoing through the empty factory. Trevor and his men dragged Isabella back to her makeshift cell, throwing her inside and locking the door behind her. She lay on the cold floor, her mind racing with fear and desperation. Back at home, Devin was frantic. Isabella had been gone too long, and his calls to her phone went unanswered. He contacted Jamie, who immediately began tracking Isabella's phone. It took time, but eventually, they pinpointed its location at the abandoned factory.

Devin's heart pounded with fear and determination. He gathered a small group of trusted friends, armed themselves, and set out to rescue Isabella. As they approached the factory, a sense of dread settled over them, the ominous atmosphere heightening their anxiety. They moved cautiously through the darkened corridors, their senses on high alert. Devin's heart raced as they neared the area where Isabella was being held. He could hear muffled voices and the sound of footsteps echoing through the factory. Devin signaled for the others to spread out, preparing for a confrontation. He moved forward, his grip on his weapon tight, his mind focused on getting Isabella out safely. As they reached the room where she was held, he saw Trevor and his men standing guard. "Trevor!" Devin shouted, stepping into the open. "Let her go!" Trevor turned, a cruel smile spreading across his face. "Devin, I was wondering when you'd show up."

The tension in the room was palpable, the air thick with anticipation. Devin took a step forward, his eyes locked on Trevor. "This ends now, Trevor." Trevor laughed, a dark, menacing sound. "You think you can stop me? You're a fool, Devin. You have no idea what you're up against." Devin's grip tightened on his weapon. "I know enough. And I know I'm not leaving here without Isabella." Trevor's smile faded, replaced by a look of cold fury. "Then you're going to die here, Devin." The room erupted into chaos as gunfire filled the air. Devin and his friends fought fiercely, their determination to save Isabella driving them forward. The battle was intense, the sounds of struggle echoing through the factory.

Devin fought his way through Trevor's men, his heart pounding with fear and desperation. He had to reach Isabella. He couldn't let Trevor win. As he fought, his thoughts were consumed with memories of their life together, their love, their children. He couldn't lose her. Finally, he broke through, reaching the door to Isabella's cell. He kicked it open, his heart leaping with relief as he saw her inside. "Bella!" Isabella's eyes widened with relief and fear. "Devin! Be careful!" He rushed to her side, untying her restraints and helping her to her feet. "We have to get out of here, now." As they moved to escape, Trevor appeared in the doorway, his face twisted with rage. "You're not going anywhere, Isabella." Devin stepped in front of her, his weapon raised. "You're not taking her, Trevor."

Trevor lunged forward, and the two men clashed, their fight brutal and desperate. Devin's strength was fueled by his love for Isabella, his determination to protect her at all costs. The struggle was fierce, but eventually, Devin gained the upper hand, knocking Trevor to the ground. He grabbed Isabella's hand, pulling her towards the exit. "Come on, we have to go!" They ran through the factory, the sounds of gunfire and shouts echoing around them. Devin's friends covered their escape, holding off Trevor's men as they made their way to safety. As they burst out of the factory and into the night, Isabella felt a rush of relief and gratitude. They had made it. They were free. But the danger was far from over. Victor Kane was still out there, and he wouldn't stop until he got what he wanted. Devin held Isabella close, his heart pounding with a mixture of fear and determination. "We'll get through this, Bella. Together." Isabella nodded, her resolve steeling. "Together."

14

Into the Shadows

Devin and Isabella burst out of the factory, the cold night air hitting them like a wave. The sense of relief was short-lived as Devin heard footsteps approaching rapidly from behind. He turned just in time to see Victor Kane emerge from the shadows; his face twisted with a sinister grin.

Before Devin could react, Victor lunged forward, grabbing Isabella and yanking her away from Devin. She screamed; her voice filled with terror as she struggled against Victor's iron grip. "Isabella!" Devin shouted, his heart pounding with fear and rage. Victor's eyes glinted with a cruel amusement. "Did you really think you could escape so easily?" Devin lunged at Victor, but he was intercepted by Trevor, who tackled him to the ground. The impact knocked the wind out of him, and he struggled to regain his breath as Trevor pinned him down. "Not so fast, Devin," Trevor sneered, his voice dripping with hate. "We're not done yet." Devin fought against Trevor's hold, his desperation fueling his strength. But Trevor was relentless, delivering a sharp blow to Devin's head that left him dazed and disoriented. He felt his wrists being bound tightly behind his back, the ropes cutting into his skin. "Devin!" Isabella's voice was filled with panic as she watched Trevor tie Devin up. She kicked and fought against Victor, but his grip was unyielding. Victor leaned in close to her ear, his voice a cold whisper. "Struggle all you want, Isabella. It won't change any thing."

Devin's vision blurred as he tried to focus on Isabella. "Let her go, Victor. This is between us." Victor chuckled; the sound without any warmth. "Oh, it's very much about her, Devin. You just don't understand yet." With Devin securely tied up, Trevor and Victor dragged him back into the factory, forcing Isabella to follow. The harsh atmosphere of the abandoned building seemed to close in around them, the darkness amplifying their fear. They were taken to a large, dimly lit room, the walls echoing with their footsteps. Trevor pushed Devin into a chair, securing him with more ropes while Victor held Isabella close, his grip never wavering. "What do you want, Victor?" Isabella demanded, her voice trembling with a mix of fear and defiance. "Why are you doing this?" Victor smiled, a cold, calculating expression. "You have no idea how valuable you are, Isabella. Or the role you play in my plans."

Devin struggled against his restraints, his eyes blazing with fury. "If you hurt her, I swear—" "Save your threats, Devin," Victor interrupted, his tone mocking. "You're in no position to make demands." Trevor stood beside Devin; his eyes filled with a sadistic pleasure. "It's time you learned the truth, Devin. About who you've been dealing with." Victor's smile widened. "You see, Isabella, you are the key to unlocking a very important door. A door that leads to immense power and influence." Isabella's brow furrowed in confusion. "What are you talking about?" Victor's eyes gleamed with a twisted satisfaction. "Your family has connections, Isabella. Connections that go back generations. Your father was involved in something much bigger than you could ever imagine." Devin's heart sank as he listened, his mind racing to piece together the puzzle. "What do you mean?"

Victor's gaze shifted to Devin, his expression darkening. "Isabella's father was part of an elite group, a shadowy organization that wields incredible power behind the scenes. They control everything from politics to finance, and your father was one of their key players." Isabella's eyes widened in shock. "My father... he was involved in something like that?" Victor nodded. "He was, and now that he's gone, the organization sees you as his successor. They believe you hold the key to accessing their secrets." Devin's blood ran cold. "And you want to use her to gain control of this organization?" Victor's smile was lacking any warmth. "Exactly. With Isabella under my control, I can unlock the secrets of the organization and seize the power they hold. But first, I need her to cooperate." Isabella's heart pounded with fear and disbelief. "I won't help you, Victor. No matter what you do." Victor's expression hardened. "You will, Isabella. Because if you don't, I will make sure everyone you care about suffers. Starting with Devin." Devin's anger flared, his muscles straining against the ropes. "Don't you dare touch her, Victor."

Victor's eyes gleamed with a cold menace. "Oh, I won't have to. You see, I have something else planned for you, Devin. Something that will ensure Isabella's cooperation." He nodded to Trevor, who approached Devin with a cruel smile. "It's time for you to learn what happens to those who stand in our way." Trevor raised his fist, delivering a brutal punch to Devin's face. The impact sent pain radiating through Devin's skull, but he refused to cry out. He wouldn't give them the satisfaction. Isabella screamed, tears streaming down her face. "Stop! Please, stop hurting him!" Victor's smile was icy. "You can make this stop, Isabella. All you have to do is cooperate." Devin's vision blurred as he struggled to stay conscious. He could feel the blood trickling down his face, but his focus remained on Isabella. "Don't... listen to him, Bella." Victor's patience seemed to wane. "Trevor, make sure he understands the consequences of defiance."

Trevor's fists continued to rain down on Devin, each blow more vicious than the last. Devin's body ached with every strike, but his spirit remained unbroken. He wouldn't let them win. Finally, Victor held up a hand, signaling Trevor to stop. "Enough. I think he's learned his lesson." Devin's head lolled to the side, his breaths coming in ragged gasps. He could barely see through the haze of pain, but he could still hear Isabella's anguished cries. Victor turned to Isabella, his expression cold and calculating. "Do you see what happens when you defy me, Isabella? This is just a taste of what I can do." Isabella's heart broke at the sight of Devin's battered form. She felt a surge of anger and determination. "You're a monster, Victor."

Victor's smile was chilling. "I prefer to think of myself as a realist. Now, are you ready to cooperate, or do I need to make an example of someone else?" Isabella's mind raced, the weight of the situation pressing down on her. She couldn't let Victor hurt anyone else. She had to find a way to stop him. "I'll cooperate," she said, her voice trembling but resolute. "Just... don't hurt anyone else." Victor's smile widened. "Good. That's the spirit. Now, let's get to work." As Trevor untied Devin, Victor kept a close eye on Isabella, ensuring she didn't try anything foolish. Devin struggled to stand, his body bruised and battered, but his eyes burned with a fierce determination. "I'm not done with you, Victor," Devin growled, his voice hoarse. "I'll find a way to stop you." Victor's smile was cold. "You're welcome to try, Devin. But remember, I hold all the cards now."

As they were led deeper into the factory, Isabella's mind raced with thoughts of escape and revenge. She couldn't let Victor win. She had to find a way to stop him and protect her family. The shadows closed in around them, the factory's crushing atmosphere amplifying their sense of dread. But even in the darkness, there was a flicker of hope. Isabella and Devin had faced impossible odds before, and they would do it again. Together. As they were forced into a new room, Victor's plan began to unfold. He outlined his demands, detailing how Isabella would help him unlock the secrets of the organization her father had been a part of. Isabella listened, her mind working tirelessly to find a way out of this nightmare. But as Victor spoke, a chilling realization settled over her. This wasn't just about power or control. It was personal. Victor had a vendetta, a grudge that went beyond mere ambition. And Isabella was at the center of it.

Devin's grip on her hand tightened, a silent promise that they would get through this. They had faced monsters before, and they had always come out stronger. This time would be no different. Victor's voice droned on, but Isabella's mind was already forming a plan. She would bide her time, gather information, and when the moment was right, she would strike. She would protect her family, no matter the cost. As the night wore on, the sense of dread never lifted. The factory's shadows seemed to close in around them, a constant reminder of the danger they faced. But even in the darkest moments, there was a spark of hope. Isabella and Devin had each other. And together, they would find a way to overcome the darkness that threatened to consume them. The battle was far from over, but they were ready to face whatever came next. As the door to their makeshift prison closed behind them, Isabella looked at Devin, her eyes filled with determination. "We'll get through this, Devin. I promise." Devin nodded, his grip on her hand firm and reassuring. "Together, Bella. Always together."

15

Shadows and Light

The sun had fully risen, casting long shadows over the abandoned factory. The aftermath of the night's events lingered like a dense fog, refusing to lift. Devin and Isabella held each other tightly, their hearts heavy with the weight of what they had just endured. But a gnawing sense of unfinished business continued, a feeling that the worst was not yet over. Devin's injuries, though not life-threatening, were severe enough to warrant immediate medical attention. An ambulance arrived, and paramedics quickly attended to him. Isabella stayed by his side, her hand gripping his tightly, refusing to let go. The chaos around them felt distant, muted by the overwhelming relief that they were still together. As the paramedics worked, Jamie approached, his expression grave. "We've got Trevor and Victor in custody. They won't be causing any more trouble."

Isabella nodded, but her gut told her it wasn't over. There was a lingering tension in the air, an unease that suggested more was to come. She looked at Devin, his eyes filled with determination despite his pain. "We need to stay vigilant, Bella. They have connections. This might not be the end." Devin was loaded into the ambulance, and Isabella climbed in beside him. As they sped towards the hospital, her mind raced with possibilities, every bump in the road a reminder of the treacherous journey they had endured. In the hospital, doctors and nurses buzzed around Devin, assessing his injuries. Isabella sat by his bedside, holding his hand, whispering words of encouragement. She felt a deep sense of gratitude for his strength and resilience. But her thoughts were interrupted by a sudden commotion outside the room. A nurse rushed in, her face pale. "We need to move you both to a secure location. There's been a breach." Fear surged through Isabella as she looked at Devin. "What does that mean? Are we in danger?" The nurse nodded. "We're not taking any chances. Please, follow me."

Isabella and Devin were quickly moved to a secure wing of the hospital, guarded by armed officers. The sense of dread grew stronger, an ominous feeling that something terrible was about to happen. Devin, despite his injuries, remained alert, his eyes scanning the room for any sign of danger. Hours passed; the tension thick in the air. Isabella couldn't shake the feeling that they were being watched, that their enemies were still out there, waiting for the right moment to strike. As night fell, the hospital was eerily quiet, the only sound the steady beeping of machines monitoring Devin's condition. Suddenly, the lights flickered, and the power went out. The room was plunged into darkness, and Isabella's heart raced. "Devin, are you okay?" Devin's voice was steady but strained. "I'm fine, Bella. Stay close." They heard footsteps approaching, slow and deliberate. The door creaked open, and a figure stood silhouetted against the dim emergency lighting. It was Trevor, his face twisted with rage and determination. "Did you really think it would be that easy?" Trevor sneered, stepping into the room. "I'm not done with you yet, Isabella. This ends tonight." Isabella's breath caught in her throat as she moved to shield Devin. "Trevor, this is madness. It's over. You've lost."

Trevor shook his head, a manic gleam in his eyes. "Not until I get what I want. Not until you're mine." Before Isabella could react, Trevor lunged at her, but Devin, with a surge of strength, tackled him to the ground. The two men fought, the sound of their struggle filling the room. Isabella frantically looked around for something to use as a weapon, her heart pounding in her chest. Devin managed to pin Trevor down, his voice a low growl. "You'll never get her, Trevor. This ends now." Trevor's laughter was chilling. "You think you can protect her? You're weak, Devin. And you always will be." With a sudden burst of energy, Trevor threw Devin off and reached into his jacket, pulling out a knife. Isabella screamed, but before she could move, Trevor slashed at Devin, the blade slicing through flesh. Devin collapsed, blood spreading across his shirt. "No!" Isabella cried, rushing to Devin's side. "Devin, stay with me. Please."

Devin's eyes were filled with pain, but he managed to speak. "Bella, I love you. Remember that." Isabella felt a surge of anger and desperation. She turned to Trevor, her eyes blazing with fury. "You won't get away with this." Trevor smiled coldly. "We'll see about that." At that moment, Jamie burst into the room, gun drawn. "Drop the knife, Trevor!" Trevor hesitated, and in that split second, Jamie fired. The bullet hit Trevor in the shoulder, causing him to drop the knife and collapse to the floor, writhing in pain. Officers rushed in, restraining Trevor and securing the room. Isabella cradled Devin, tears streaming down her face. "Stay with me, Devin. Please." Paramedics rushed in, working quickly to stabilize Devin and stop the bleeding. Jamie knelt beside Isabella, his expression a mix of sorrow and determination. "He's going to make it, Isabella. He has to."

Hours passed in a blur of medical procedures and anxious waiting. Isabella stayed by Devin's side, her heart heavy with fear and hope. Finally, a doctor approached, his expression somber. "Mrs. Marcelli, your husband is stable for now. But his injuries are severe. The next 24 hours will be critical." Isabella nodded, her resolve firm. "I'll stay with him. No matter what." As she sat by Devin's bedside, holding his hand, she thought about the journey they had been on, the trials they had faced. She knew their love was strong enough to overcome anything, but the uncertainty of the future loomed over her like a dark cloud. Suddenly, the monitors began to beep erratically. Nurses and doctors rushed in, working frantically to stabilize Devin. Isabella's heart pounded as she watched, praying for a miracle. Time seemed to stretch, each second an eternity. Finally, the monitors returned to a steady rhythm, and the medical team stepped back, their expressions relieved. The doctor turned to Isabella, his voice gentle. "He's a fighter, Mrs. Marcelli. He's going to pull through."

Relief washed over Isabella, but the sense of dread remained. She knew the battle was not yet over, that there were still threats lurking in the shadows. But for now, she focused on Devin, on their love and their determination to face whatever came their way. Days turned into weeks, and Devin slowly began to recover. The support of their friends and family, along with the relentless pursuit of justice by Jamie and the authorities, brought a sense of security back into their lives. Trevor and Victor were finally behind bars, their reign of terror brought to an end. But as they sat together one evening, watching the sunset from their balcony, Isabella couldn't shake the feeling that the shadows of the past were never truly gone. She knew they had to remain vigilant, to protect their family from any future threats. As the final rays of the sun dipped below the horizon, Devin turned to Isabella, his eyes filled with love and determination. "We've been through so much, Bella. But we'll face whatever comes next together." Isabella nodded, her heart swelling with love for the man beside her. "Together, Devin. Always."

And as they held each other, the darkness that had once threatened to consume them seemed to fade away, replaced by a glimmer of hope and the promise of a brighter future. They had faced the shadows and emerged stronger; their love unbreakable. But deep in the recesses of her mind, Isabella knew that the battle was never truly over. There would always be challenges, always be threats lurking in the shadows. But with Devin by her side, she felt ready to face whatever came their way. For now, they held onto their love, their hope, and the promise of a future filled with endless possibilities. And as they watched the stars together, they knew that they would face the shadows together, no matter what. And somewhere, in the darkness, a figure watched, waiting for the right moment to strike. The story was far from over, and the shadows still loomed large. But for Isabella and Devin, their love remained a guiding light, illuminating the path ahead.

The end... for now.

Milton Keynes UK
Ingram Content Group UK Ltd.
UKHW020053260824
447288UK00011B/388